Knocking
BOOTS

WILLOW WINTERS

Knocking
BOOTS

Prologue

Charlie

"Charlie..."

Grace's soft voice beckons me from across the hotel room as I shut the door. I pull at the knot in my necktie, loosening it before tossing it on the floor. Through the dim light the night provides I can barely see as she scissors her legs under the stark white hotel comforter.

It's unreal to me still that she wants me so much and what's more, they all think she's *mine*. Every one of those guests at my sister's wedding thinks Grace belongs to me. Then again, the whole damn town is convinced she's the next one to get hitched.

They're right about one thing. She'll be screaming my name tonight. *But the rest is all a lie.*

"Don't make me wait anymore..." she pleads.

Grace's slender neck arches as she grips the comforter in her hands and groans out her words with a little pout on her lush lips.

I've got her so worked up, my little sweetheart, but that wasn't hard to do. I knew she wanted me. She doesn't want to *keep* me though; she just wants me for the night. Tonight, she's all mine. I'm not the kind of guy who's good enough for her. Even though my throat gets tight at the thought, and my steps pause on the way to her, I blame myself. She was too tempting to resist and all of this is my fault.

Grace isn't the kind of girl who winds up with a man like me. She's got her life planned out. She wants the whole nine yards, and in less than a year.

She wants a picture-perfect family and a white picket fence, but that's not a life I'm ready for nor one I can provide. Not right now. Maybe not ever.

I can see Grace wearing a white dress. *A wedding* dress. I bet she'd wear one of those big ass gowns with a train that fills the aisle. It's not hard to imagine how the dress would move around her long, shapely legs.

The thought of her walking down the aisle to someone else, a man other than myself, pisses me off. The anger rises, heating my blood just thinking about it and that tightness in my throat comes back with a vengeance. But there's no way in hell I'll be the man she's walking toward. We both know that. I have Grace for tonight, and that's all that matters. It's what I wanted in our deal.

It was a drunken deal we made when our flirtatious natures got out of hand. She promised to come to the wedding and pretend to be my girlfriend, to keep my family off my back.

I slip off my shirt, and start undoing my belt just as she turns onto her side and looks at me through her long lashes, her eyes shining with lust.

"I want you, Charlie." She whispers the words I've been dreaming of since she first stepped into my life.

Fuck. I can't take my name sounding like lust on her lips. As if the taste of my name is all she needs to get off.

Or maybe I'm just imagining it. Maybe all this is in my head, because I want to think that hooking up somehow means more to her now.

It wasn't supposed to be anything serious.

It was just a date. Just a release. *All of this was only for fun.* And I know after tonight, she'll be long gone.

The bed groans as I climb on top of it and I bend down to kiss the soft skin on the tender side of her neck, I can't help thinking she feels so right. So perfect in my arms.

I pull back the comforter, revealing the lacy negligee she's wearing, and watch a beautiful pink blush travel up her chest and into her cheeks.

"What's this?" I ask her with a cocked brow. My already hard dick twitches with the need to get that lingerie off of her and onto the floor. I want what's underneath.

She bites down on her bottom lip and attempts to throw back one of those smart ass responses she's always got for me, but my lips are on hers before she gets a single word out. Nipping and sucking and reveling in what's to come.

Her fingers spear into my hair and she deepens the kiss, wrapping her legs around my hips. My hands roam up the curve of her waist and back down as she moans into my mouth.

This is dangerous. I'm fucking addicted. I swear, it wasn't supposed to happen like this.

As I stare down at her beautiful face, her lips parted and her gorgeous baby blues half-lidded, I know this isn't just a good time anymore. Not for me.

I'm not the type of man she wants. We both know that. I don't have what it takes to keep her.

But damn... I want to.

Chapter
ONE

Grace

Rewinding to the beginning of this story....

"It's not the worst news, but I know it's not what you wanted to hear. Honestly though, Grace, there are a number of options," Dr. Abrahams tells me but all I can hear is the last option she gave me. The best option according to her: freezing my eggs. She smiles at me, brushing a strand of gray hair behind her ear. My own simper falters and I hate that I can't hide the disappointment better.

Looking past her at the wall I note that it's plastered with what must be hundreds of pictures of newborns who Dr. Abrahams has helped other women conceive. Their little smiles and bows and cute little fingers and toes stare back at me. The photos are framed with pink and blue paper and give the room a hopeful atmosphere. I should be more thankful;

the doctor just told me my eggs are still viable, after all. But she's given me news that a woman at my age shouldn't be getting. 'Premenopausal' isn't a word I ever thought I'd hear. Let alone this soon.

My parents always said, career first. *"Figure out your life and make sure you're stable before settling down. You have plenty of time for marriage and babies."* I suppose my father didn't think I'd be premenopausal either.

Barely keeping the smile on my face, I nod at whatever Dr. Abrahams said although I have no idea what came out of her mouth.

All isn't lost yet, but if I don't act soon my chances of having a child will be gone. Even now, without IVF, the odds are slim. My hormones have just given up apparently.

I'm only thirty. So... I've got to meet someone, and get him to propose. That's a year and a half, optimistically. Hopefully it's someone who wants to have kids, with extensive and expensive medical help more than likely. My mind drifts back to my health insurance and I wonder what's covered and what's not.

They say that people who wait at least three years before tying the knot stay married longer, so that's three years longer I'd have to wait. Then there's conception and gestation... and the birth, of course. My fingers run circles around each other, twiddling as I think of how this is possible. It has to be possible though, because I've always wanted a child. The thought of a bundled up newborn with a little button nose and sweet yawn takes over for a moment and my throat goes dry as my eyes prick. I can't not have a child. I nearly say the words out loud but somehow I keep them down. Swallowing them and reminding myself that freezing my eggs will work. The doctor said so.

The little plan in my head means it will be more than five years and thousands of dollars before any baby could be a reality, assuming everything goes perfectly. *If* the IVF works on the first try. My gaze drifts to the wall of babies, which seems to be mocking me.

"Grace," Dr. Abrahams says gently, reaching across her desk to touch my hand. The sudden touch is jolting, bringing me back to the present. My very single, very baby-less present. "Did you hear me? I have some pamphlets here for the fertility preservation clinics I recommend."

She presents a number of brightly colored brochures, waiting for me to take them and smiles.

"Okay?" My answer comes out as a question, rather than any kind of statement. This isn't at all what I expected from my checkup. To say I'm shocked is an understatement. "Thank you," I quickly add and hope that she didn't take my initial response as rude. Clearing my throat, I smile broadly. "I appreciate it," I tell her and somehow my voice is even and echoes a happiness that's absent from how I truly feel.

"We have your follow-up visit scheduled," the doctor says absently, clicking the keys on her computer and staring at the screen, "so you're all set." She finally looks at me with a smile.

I can't return it as I nod my head. A follow up in a few days to see how bad it is. *How bad.* Not if it's okay. But *how bad.* She didn't use that exact term but it's what she meant. Once the blood work is done she can tell me just *how bad* it is.

Just wonderful. *I can hardly wait,* my inner voice is deadpan and again I keep my mouth shut.

"If you have any further questions, don't hesitate to call."

I manage a smile, nodding and when she stands, I do too, gripping my purse with both clammy hands.

A nurse in hot pink scrubs whisks me out to the reception

area. "Have a nice day, Miss Campbell," she tells me, winking before she turns to call her next patient amongst the women seated there. "Mrs. Gray? Shellie Gray?"

"Here!" A woman who looks to be in her early forties with kind wrinkles around her deep brown eyes pushes herself to her feet.

I drift out of the woman's way, and then the nurse closes the door behind them both. I take a deep breath, giving myself a mental shake, and head out to the parking lot. The pictures of all those babies playing in front of my eyes.

My mind is awhirl with thoughts, most of them depressing. More and more depressing with every step I take. I climb in my white sedan and pull the seatbelt on. With the click of the ignition, the car rumbles to life and I instantly turn the radio off, leaving just the hum of the car to accompany me before pulling out of the parking lot. The downtown Atlanta traffic is just as heavy as my thoughts.

As I sit in traffic on I-85, I stare at the Atlanta skyline. The sun is already setting against the brick buildings. The burned orange and yellow against the blue is peaceful. I sigh. The city was so fun when I was in college, and a great place to be when I was a recent graduate looking for my first serious job. No more retail and interning. No more clubs with my girlfriends and late nights that end up in horrific hangovers.

Now I have a steady, long-term career as a graphic designer in Buckhead and more and more often, I find myself driving to the suburbs. My cramped apartment in Candler Park would be left behind for the easy, laidback lifestyle I've found in Vinings, just outside the city's perimeter if I could afford the move, and the time to actually move. The thought of moving is just one more stressor to deal with. I'm pretty certain the doctor just gave me plenty to stress over.

With my fingers tapping along the leather steering wheel, traffic finally moves at a reasonable pace.

Come to think of it, I haven't even been at my apartment for more than a night's sleep or a shower in ages. I haven't been anywhere in the city, really. The nightlife doesn't call to me anymore. It's all work, work, work. I basically live at work, and that's it.

Well that and my go to bar. Everyone deserves a drink after a long day.

At the moment, all I want is to get lost in a cosmo or martini to finish this day off. And I know just where I want to have that drink —at the hole-in-the-wall bar my coworker Ann showed me a couple of months ago. Mac's bar has a jukebox, plenty of places to sit, and unlike the other bars in Vinings, it serves liquor as well as beer.

Just thinking about it has me parched. Well, that and the bartender, Charlie.

Charlie.

The traffic finally frees up completely, and I'm quick to engage the turn signal and get off at the next exit to drive toward the bar. Maybe Charlie will be there. He usually is and when I get a drink or two in, he's my confidant. That thought puts a smile on my face. It's nice to have someone to talk to and as much as Ann is a good friend for gossip, that's essentially all she does. Gossip.

I jump out of the car in the parking lot of Mac's Tavern, and look at my reflection in the side of the car. Brilliant blue eyes lined with kohl, long waves of copper-colored hair, and a cute upturned nose greet me. If I was nitpicky, I'd say that my eyes are a little too big, that my lips are too wide.

But I'm trying to get away from that kind of thinking. I tug my pale yellow skirt down and undo a button on my collar. There's no one to impress inside Mac's, so it's time to get comfy.

After fluffing my hair once, I lock my car and head inside. The place is an old brick building, plain and short. Stepping inside is like a breath of fresh air, when you crave a break from it all. There's an ancient wooden bar along one side of the room, plenty of stools, chairs and tables to fill up the space with the exception of a small dance area that remains clear. It's dimly lit, but that's just fine by me because it aids in the pub atmosphere.

The sound of balls knocking together on the pool table in the back and the chatter of people follow me to the bar. I prefer it to a table. You never know who you're going to meet at the bar or what stories you'll hear. That's mostly what Charlie and I talk about. The regulars, their drama and anything else new in this part of town.

It's nice to unwind like that.

As I make my way to the bar, I realize that I'm smiling. There's something about this place that does that to me. There are about a dozen people sprinkled throughout the bar, mostly enjoying after-work drinks.

I walk right over to the bar and sit down at the very end. *It's my seat.* I look down the bar, but find the area behind it is empty. I wonder where the bartender is. There's one special guy who could make today complete… *if* he's working, that is.

Then a back door swings open, revealing *him*. Charlie, the owner of this bar.

He's tall and broad-shouldered, with light brown hair cropped close to his scalp. He's wearing a blue plaid shirt and jeans, but that doesn't stop me from staring at his rippling muscles as he moves a stack of heavy-looking boxes behind the bar. Along with a jawline made for women to swoon over and twin brows that raise and lower with every emotion, he's got a nose that's just *too* perfect. It fits so well with his physique.

I bite my lip and blush. I know Charlie isn't for me, really I do. I literally just found out that my time is running out to form a real connection with someone. It's just... well, Charlie is *hot*.

The kind of hot that might keep a girl up at night, wondering just what's under those jeans. Wondering if he's as stacked as you hope he is...

If the other girls hanging around and looking at him wistfully are anything to go by, Charlie's packing some serious heat. Then again, none of those girls have managed to nail him down.

And none of them were walking around, thinking of baby names in their spare time. Yep, I need to keep my hands to myself. My eyes, however...

A pleasant sigh leaves me as Charlie turns and sets the boxes down, giving me a good shot of his ass. It's perfect, nice and round. I swear, I never even noticed things like that before I met Charlie.

I chew my lip as I lean forward just a hair wondering if he does a lot of squats at the gym, or if his bubble butt is natural. Okay, maybe this is a little too much. Sitting back on the stool, I shake off my over active hormones and remind myself that he's just a guy that is a part of this safe space I've made for myself to unwind.

He turns around just as I'm nodding to myself and catches me still looking at his rear. "Hey, stranger."

Shit. I blush deep red, because I forgot the most stunning thing about Charlie: his eyes. They're a kind of moss green color, something straight out of National Geographic.

"Hey," I manage, the single word somehow coming out as two syllables, and I break off eye contact. I realize that my crush on Charlie is all it will ever be, a crush. I need to stop being such a weirdo.

I make eye contact again.

"Where have you been? It's been a whole week since I've seen your face around here," he teases.

"Oh. Just work," I say with a shrug. "You know, the usual."

"Yeah?" he says, grabbing a small worn hand towel and wiping off his hands. "That's it, huh?"

"That's it."

His voice drops as he leans against the bar. "Nothing interesting to report?"

Somehow, he manages to make that sound filthy. God help me. There's a charm about his raised brow and the way he looks expectantly at me. The fluttering in my chest needs to quit it.

"Nope." I push my hair back off my shoulders, feeling a little hotter than I should.

"Too bad. I was looking forward to you telling me some tales." He looks down the bar and nods to someone he knows. "Can I get you something to drink?"

"Umm… something chilled with vodka but tastes fruity."

"You got it." With a pat on the bar from him, I smile broadly. That's one of the reasons I love being here.

He moves down the bar to fulfill my order, and I nearly groan to see him go.

Yeah, it's safe to say that I'm holding a bit of a torch for him. I know he's not what I want —he's hot, but completely allergic to commitment. It's why I've never approached him like that. He knows I'm on the prowl, as he says, for a husband and someone to settle away from the city with. As he's told me before, he has no intention of settling down. Still, there's no law against looking, is there?

My chin fits right into place in the palm of my hand and I sigh to myself while I stare after him.

Chapter
TWO

Charlie

W ell, my day just got a whole lot better. Grace is one of my regulars, and a favorite customer. It helps that she's hot as hell. I smirk as I fill the shaker with a shot of vodka and then a bit more and set the bottle back on ice behind the bar. Her smile's a little weak but a drink or two and her sweet feminine laugh will come out easy enough.

"Charlie," Mickey calls out to me. He's another regular and the uncle of one of my employees.

I give him a nod, grabbing a tall glass and throwing the handle for the Guinness back to get Mickey another. He'll be here all night, staring up at the college games on the televisions above me.

There are plenty of regulars, some of them like family. Grace isn't like that. I don't know how to describe her to be honest. I just know I like it when she's here.

I slide him the beer, scooting it across the bar top. I'm half tempted to ask him where the hell his nephew is since he never showed up for work, but it's not like he'd know. The bar is just outside the city and located in a small town. Bringing up business to Mickey isn't going to help any. He's a retired cop, and his wife passed away from cancer not too long ago. I'm not going to give him a hard time because his nephew doesn't have a clue what work ethic is.

"Thank you, sir," Mickey tells me, grabbing his beer. He doesn't even look away from the game on television. Beer, football, and a crowded place keep him sane and help him deal with it all.

"Charlie!" Maggie calls out from behind me. She swings open the doors to the back and walks through as she throws on her apron. Thank fuck she's here.

"Is the kitchen all set?" she asks. She puts her arms around her back, as she ties the apron.

"Yeah, it should be ready for you," I tell her, grabbing the short iced down glass for Grace. I try to fight back my agitation.

James is really looking to be fired. I've absolutely had it with him getting drunk after closing and not showing up the next day. He's young and stupid. I know what that lifestyle is like, since I used to be just like him, but I'm sick and tired of putting up with his shit.

I didn't hire him so I could do the work of two men when one doesn't show.

I'm fucking exhausted, and the night's just getting started. But that's what this business takes. Hard work and dedication. It's not what I thought it'd be when I opened a bar at the outskirts of town. I know part of the reason I did it was to get away.

Part of it was to drown out the memory of the past with booze.

That was years ago though when I was dumb and stupid. Somehow I got lucky, and this damn bar is the only good thing I've got going for me now. I can't let a little shithead like James screw things up.

"Thanks for coming in, Mags."

I turn to look over my shoulder, but Maggie's already gone. She's a hard ass and doesn't need to be given praise, but I should give her a raise or a bonus. Good help's hard to find in a small town where people think they can get away with this shit.

"Citrus and peach tonight?" I ask Grace.

I set the glass in front of her and wipe my hand off on my faded blue jeans. Her slender fingers brush against mine as she takes the glass with both her hands.

"Sounds delicious to me," she says with a hint of a blush to her cheeks. "I need it." I cock my head at her, waiting for her to elaborate.

"Things going okay?" She asks as her brows pinch, and she looks past me to the swinging double doors Mags went through. "Not that I'm trying to change the subject or anything... you just seem like something's off."

I shrug and lean my hip against the bar as I pick up a rag to wipe things down. I let out a deep breath and try to shrug it off, but Grace looks at me pointedly, taking a sip and smiling before setting the glass down. I don't know why, but it makes me smile too.

"It's really good," she tells me and sways slightly. She does that, rocking gently when she decides to get comfortable.

"A new hire didn't show up is all," I answer Grace without thinking.

I'm relaxed as I do a quick scan, making sure no one's glass is empty and I've taken care of everyone so far who's come in. Rick will be here soon to help and with Mags in the back we should be good for tonight, but the last two hours have been hell doing it all on my own. The wet rag in my hand glides down the bar easily, soaking up the spilled beer. I sealed and lacquered the oak bar myself. This bar is my baby. And James doesn't respect it, or his job.

"Uh oh," she answers playfully and I give her a scolding look that grants me a laugh from her. "I'd be pissed too," she says finally.

She smiles into her glass when I grunt a response and prepare another beer for a customer in the back.

My gaze lifts to Grace's as she hums; her warm breath creates a fog on it before she takes a sip. She moans soft and sweet, loving the taste. I know it's an innocent move on her part, but I'll be damned if it doesn't make my dick hard as stone.

Grace has got something about her that makes her easy to talk to. Maybe it's because she's not from around here, so I know nothing I say is going to be used against me later on. People in this town talk, and it drives me up the damn wall.

It takes a moment to drop the beer off and ask the other patrons if they're doing alright or if they need anything.

"You going to fire him?" she asks when I finally get back to Grace.

Her fingers slip up and down creating a line in the dew of her glass. I don't think she's doing it intentionally, but that simple innocuous movement is making my already hard dick twitch with need. I've had plenty of nights to try to take her home, but those nights have held conversations about what she's looking for in a man and how she's finally wanting to settle down.

AKA exactly the reason I don't want to take her home. It would kill me if we hooked up and she had regrets about it. We're friends in the making. Nothing more.

My head shakes at her question; I don't trust myself to speak. I wouldn't fire James. His aunt was one of my teachers all throughout high school. His parents live not five houses down from my parents. Little shit knows it, too.

"Well maybe you should make him wash the dishes when he comes in then," she answers with a shrug that makes her buttoned-up blouse slip open just slightly. "Or have him rearrange all the boxes in the back?"

I can't help that my eyes dart down to her cleavage even as I chuckle at her suggestion. It's a modest top, probably perfect for that office job she's got. But right now, it's giving me a teasing glimpse and I want to see more.

"I am-" I tell her as I see Mickey waving me down. "Soon as he gets in here, no bartending, all dishes and grunt work." I'm half playing, half-serious. The grill in the back needs to be scrubbed down, along with all the equipment, and that's James' payback. That and I have to cut back his hours until I'm sure he'll actually show up during rush hours. She laughs that sweet, soft sound I know is genuine. I tap the bar with a smile as I walk to the other end to Mickey.

"Can you get me some wings?" he says as he pats his stomach. His shirt strains as he stretches backward. The buttons on his shirt gape and are showing a bit too much but only when he stretches back.

"Ranch on the side?"

He nods, "That'll do it."

"Course, Mickey." I open the double doors just a touch and call out to Mags. "An order of wings, hot."

I look back to make sure Mickey wants his usual. This

bar's become a routine for him, just like it has for a lot of the town.

He nods his head, and I don't even hesitate to walk right back to Grace. It's become a natural habit of mine when she's here.

Most of the guys in here want to get away. They want a place to watch the games, to drink, to chat with their friends they came with. Grace comes alone most of the time. She sits by herself, and I'm the only one she talks to unless someone sidles up beside her. I like it that way. It's like she comes here just for me.

Inwardly I scoff at myself and remember a number of nights where she seemed to make best of friends with a stranger for an hour or two.

She wants company, to talk, to laugh, to forget about all her problems. I want that too.

That's all it's ever going to be though. She's told me more than once about the dates she's been on and the guys she's meeting up with. And not a damn one of them is a country boy with a reputation like mine.

I think she knows enough about all the shit I've been through. The whole damn town does… although, she's not from Vinings, so I don't think she knows the whole story. Plus, she's asked about my dating life before. I didn't give her much, but I told her the same thing I tell every woman. I'm not interested in settling down. Not now. Possibly not ever. I'm pretty certain I told her that on night one.

Either way, she's ready for the whole nine yards. She had no problem telling me that and making it clear she wasn't into one-night flings. Although, I'm not sure if she told me that more to remind herself, or to make me keep my distance. If it was the latter, she failed miserably. It only made me want her more. I'm not interested in all that shit she wants though. I've hardly got time for myself, let alone a family. But I fucking love flirting with her. Maybe it's because I know I can't have her. It's the challenge.

"So how's your day going?" I ask. "Hopefully better than mine."

I grab the stool from behind me and pull it closer to her to take a seat. It's dinner time now, so the evening rush won't come till later. I'm going to need my energy then.

"Eh." Grace makes a cute scrunched up face and takes another drink with her eyes closed tight.

"That bad, huh?" I ask her with a grin. I love how animated she is, how she wears her emotions on her sleeve. She really is a sweetheart.

"Yeah, it was rough," she admits, looking away.

She puts her glass back down on the bar and lets her fingertips glide along the edge and my smile falls.

Leaning back on the stool, I stretch and run my hand over my hair. "Sorry your day was shit. You need me to go have a word with your boss?"

My joke makes her smile at least, but she shakes her head gently with her eyes closed.

"I don't think that would help," she says softly and then focuses those baby blues on me. She has the kind of eyes a man can get lost in. They're a pale blue with tiny golden flecks that lure me in. She jokes, "Least I'm not doing dishes."

That's my girl.

Her voice is a bit choked up at the end though, which is unusual for her. She's quick to lift the drink to her lips, I think to try to hide it. She's been coming in here for a while. I'm getting used to looking forward to her coming in and chatting with me, but the look on her face right now is making my chest hurt for her.

"You can tell me if you want." My offer goes unanswered for a moment and I scan the room casually, not putting any pressure on her. Luckily, she starts talking before I meet her baby blues again.

"I went to the doctor today." She taps the bar as she talks, staring where her fingers play along it. "My eggs decided to boycott so I can't have kids." She takes in a shuddering breath and then rolls her eyes, playing it off and shaking her head. "Well, not the traditional way anyway. And they'll be expensive as fuck if I do have them."

"You alright?" I ask her. I watch the raw vulnerability as it's replaced with a mask of lightheartedness.

"Yeah, I'm fine. It's just unexpected." She finally looks me in the eyes as she adds, "I'm gonna start a bill for each one now so they can cover these fertility treatments. They can pay me back after they graduate." She laughs at her joke, and I let out a huff of a chuckle just to make her feel more at ease. Fuck, it hurts though to see the pain in her eyes.

"Sorry," I tell her sincerely. I've never even thought about kids. With the bar, I don't have the time, even if I wanted them.

"Don't be. I just got the news, so I'm all flustered, but I will figure it out."

"I can imagine." No I can't. But I think what I'm saying is comforting.

A few more guys and a couple come in and take me from her, but I keep my eye on her glass. I'm waiting for it to empty, so I have a reason to get back to her. The beer flows easily as the orders continue to come in. UGA is playing, and most of the bar is rooting for wins, which means Mickey buys the guys in the back a round of shots.

All the while Grace spins slightly on her stool and

occasionally checks her phone. Mostly she just stares directly ahead of her at nothing in particular, a vacant look in her eyes and her lips turned down slightly. It gets busier and busier, but all I want is for her to call me over to her or finish that last bit of her drink.

I check with her a few times, but she waves me off with a small smile. Each time she's just as welcoming and tempting as the last. But work calls, stealing me from her and leaving her alone in the bar. Every time I peek up, I see a sadness behind those big blue doe eyes that I don't like seeing.

Time passes quickly and before I know it, she's taking out her clutch and leaving cash on the bar. The second I see her put the money down, I stop pouring the draft beer in my hands and call out to her over the hum of loud voices.

"You need a ride?"

She smiles back at me and shakes her head no, but that happiness on her face makes it worth it.

I slide the beer down to the very end of the bar, forgetting which one of the two men sitting there ordered it, and walk over to check her out. I grab the cash and turn to go to the register, but she tells me to keep the change. She always does.

"Thank you, sweetheart," I tell her and watch as she spins in her seat.

"I bet you call all the ladies sweetheart," she tells me playfully, but her words are a kick to my gut.

"Just you," I tell her, trying to keep my voice chipper and not let on.

"Yeah, okay," Grace says as she tries to get off the stool. She seems a little off balance, so I make my way around to her and I'm damn glad I did. She slips off the stool and nearly stumbles. I catch her in my arms and hold her upright as she struggles to slide her small foot back into her heel. Her hands are firm on my forearms until she's got her balance back.

"I'm not tipsy, just these heels." That beautiful blush rises up her chest and into her cheeks as she shakes her head. She tries to play it off, backing out of my embrace. Her lush ass hits the stool behind her, and her hands grip onto it to keep from knocking it over. I can't help the rough chuckle from vibrating up my chest.

"You sure you don't need a ride?" I ask Grace. I know she only had one drink. I know she doesn't. That doesn't change the fact that I want to give her a ride.

"No, I'm fine," she says. There's a small smile on her face I can tell she's trying to fight.

"I don't know if I believe you." I tell her just to fuck with her. I love getting under her skin. "I wouldn't mind taking you home."

I give her a wink as I back away. Leaving her there, steady on her feet, I walk around the counter to get to unloading the boxes that fucking James was supposed to take care of. I look over my shoulder when she doesn't respond and catch her staring at my ass... again. It takes her a second before she notices my eyes on her.

Her eyes widen slightly, those beautiful baby blues looking like she knows she got caught. A violent shade of red floods her cheeks as she shakes her head, pulling her hair to one side and starts walking backward.

"I'm sure you wouldn't," she says playfully. But it's that very thought that's keeping her away from me. A woman like her, someone put together, with her life all figured out... She doesn't date men like me.

"Have a good night, sweetheart," I tell her one last time.

She waves shyly as she leaves me with nothing more than a "you too".

Yeah, I've made some mistakes in the past. I have a reputation, and I'm sure as shit not looking for the same things she is.

But I wouldn't mind knocking boots with my little sweetheart.

Chapter
THREE

Grace

I t's 3 p.m., and I have a thousand things to do at work in only two hours. It's not going to happen. That's the bottom line. I push myself back from my desk in my rolling chair and sigh while looking around my cubicle. It's littered with coffee mugs with motivational phrases, like, 'I drink coffee and I get shit done', notepads that have to do lists on them and pens. There are pens everywhere. In coffee cups, on top of to do lists and in the top drawer. Why? Because everyone takes my pens. Just like my mugs, they have cute things on them. My most recent set: keep your hands off my pens. I bought a six pack, I'm already down to four… I think… unless one is tucked in my purse or a drawer.

I'm in the advertising design department here at L. J. Scott & Co, which supposedly fulfills my need to create. The stack of ads, printed out on thick photography paper, at my right hand can attest to that.

I went to Rhode Island School of Design for marketing, with a minor in graphic design not realizing how much both subjects would challenge my creativity. I freaking love it. Eventually, I settled in at this graphic design job, choosing it over the other two offers because I like the work done here. It's as simple as that. Day in and day out I get a different task and a different market to tap into.

All but one of the checkboxes on my list have been checked off, tick, tick, tick. Just the last one remains: find a hubby and make those babies.

"Hey! Drinks after work?" a chipper voice calls out from behind me. The pen in my hand lands on my desk when I jolt back to reality. The cat on my screen licking his chops is nearly just as startling. Nothing says, 'your cat wants this kibble' like an open mouthed cat ready to devour it.

I swivel my chair around and find Diane, leaning on the wall between our cubicles. She tilts her blonde head in a come-hither sort of way. She exudes sex appeal and often unbuttons her blouse a bit too low for client orientation which has led to more than a few rumors at the water cooler so to speak. AKA it's how she wins a number of her jobs.

Diane started at the company at the same time as I did, and didn't really give me much of a choice as to whether I would be her friend.

It was more that she assumed I wanted to go get drinks after work that first day, and I went along with it, why wouldn't I? I soon found out why. She doesn't really know limits and boundaries, not with men, not with alcohol and not with personal questions. She's downright intrusive and cringe worthy when drunk, but I prefer that to sober Diane. Although in either state, she laughs a little too loud and right now I'm just not in the mood. I'm still processing everything from my doctor's visit. Unfortunately, I have a bad habit of always saying yes. She's not mean spirited, she's not a bad person. She's just… A LOT to take in. And since Ann is on leave for three months, I'll admit I'm a tad bit lonely.

"Sure," I answer, trying not to look at my desk, at the red blinking light on the phone that means I have messages. "That sounds good." I close my eyes as soon as the words come out of my mouth. I didn't even think about saying no.

"Mac's?" she asks, as if we would go anywhere else. I'm not the only one who lusts after Charlie. Diane flirts with him *big time*, counting down the days till he's in her bed.

"Sure," I say, breathing a small sigh of relief. At least it's Mac's.

"'Kay! See you at five thirty, then." Her eyes travel down my body. "I hope you brought a change of clothes. I'm planning on the two of us getting handsy with some hotties tonight," her smile dims as she rolls her eyes and adds beneath her breath, "not going to a friggin' funeral."

Boundaries, Diane. My inner voice is snappy with a comeback but I just smile. I will wear whatever the heck I want. Diane's embarrassment for me will just have to deal with it.

With that, she steps back and disappears behind the wall of her cubicle.

I blow out a breath. It wouldn't be the first time Diane has called dibs on a guy I liked, slept with one of them. Diane's a little competitive… in everything. Work's like that, too; she likes to have the biggest and best clients under her purview in sales, often promising customers off-the-wall things and then dropping the whole stack of work in someone else's lap. She did it to me when I first started… I learned quick to tell her my own workload was full.

Wheeling my way back to my desk I send up yet another

prayer for more women to be hired here or even men, so long as they're actually social and then glance at my cell phone, which is face down on my desk to keep me from getting distracted. But right now, I need the distraction. The second I click it on I see a message from Jason on Tinder. I open the app and make a face as I scan the message.

Hey there —you look beautiful. Are you free tonight?

A tingle runs down my spine as I read it and look at the guy's pictures. Oh yeah... there is *definitely* a reason I liked his profile. He's blond and handsome in the photos, and his profile says he's looking for a serious commitment.

I hesitate for only a moment, then type a message in return.

Thank you! And I am free, actually. What were you thinking? Double checking it to make sure there are no obvious signs that I haven't dated in practically forever, I send it.

Sitting a little straighter in my chair I think: maybe tonight won't be a disaster after all. Back to work I go. Time to be as much of a super woman as I can be in the final hours.

I have to return a dozen calls. Only one of them gets to me. Criticism is something I can take. I don't mind it. But when a client treats me like crap, it gets to me. I wish it didn't, but it gets to me. Sometimes this job is stressful and it's 100% the clients who lead me down one path, tweaking a design a million ways, and then wanting to trash it. They do it again and again, while deadlines slip by and they don't seem to have any grasp on what they actually want. I constantly interact with customers who want four more mock-ups than the three I've initially provided, as per their contract with L. J. Scott & Co. I'll make them a dozen if they need it. If that's what it takes to ignite a spark, I will do it all day long. But don't have me do a dozen, choose one to tweak a million times, then another, then another and waste weeks of work not deciding a damn thing and wanting to start from scratch.

Tapping my nails on the desk I take in steadying breaths and pretend like Anthony from Bike It isn't going to take every single one of those tweaked designs and use them all. I know we're expensive and he has commented such a number of times, but the package he chose isn't for a limitless number of ads and that's what I think he wants.

Of course, Diane has promised this client the moon, she had him first before our boss moved him to me, but at half the cost of the creative hours billed so far, which are now supposedly useless.

"Hey! Got you a coffee!" Tracey's voice echoes in the small cubicle. Letting out a breath I didn't know I'd been holding, I swirl around and thank her. It's impossible to be mad or sad or anything other than grateful around Tracey, the office personal assistant. Just the sound of her pushing around that cart is enough to lift my spirits.

"Anything good?" I ask, eyeing her coffee-with-cream skin and sleek, high ponytail. I'm weirdly jealous of Tracey's consistent good cheer, her youth, and her easy breezy attire. I'm even jealous of the way she wears that pale pink dress probably because she's obviously naturally skinny. She could be a model and I've told her that a million times.

"Psshh," she says, grinning as she hands me a cup. "Same thing as usual. A shot in the dark. Coffee, espresso, two creamers, and one Splenda."

"Thank you so much," I say, looking at the tiny puff of steam that escapes my cup. "I seriously need this right now."

"I got you," she says, winking. "You need anything else?"

A new client? One not from hell? Maybe some new ovaries? I think. But I stay quiet and shake my head. I'll give this guy another week and if he's still yanking me around, I have to go to the higher ups. I hate doing that, but I know my limits. There are givers and takers in this world, the givers have to have boundaries, because the takers have none. My mind flashes with an image of Diane and I shut that down with a gulp of hot coffee.

"Alright. Well I have tons of three-o'clock-slump-coffees to deliver," she says, backing her cart out of my cubicle. "See you tomorrow."

"Have a good night," I reply, turning back to my desk after saluting her with my cup.

The smell of the coffee and espresso makes my lips turn upward. Holding onto it with two hands, I take a sip and sigh with fulfillment.

Sure my job can suck when one client decides to shit on my entire day, but there's an endless coffee supply. That's gotta be worth something, right?

With only an hour left of the work day, I mouse over to Adobe Photoshop, clicking through the six ads I'm working on for other clients, ones that have given me direction I can actually use and ones I don't think are using me.

Another message from Jason makes my phone vibrate and I actually feel a hint of excitement. The corners of my lips kick up as I read:

Have you ever been to The Brick Store Pub in Decatur? They have great drinks, and the food's good, too.

I bite my lip with a nervous excitement although it's quick to dissipate when I think of exchanging a night at Mac's with Charlie for this new guy. But the new guy is looking for commitment. He's not the safe 'never-going-to-want-me-like-that Charlie' and Decatur isn't that far away from where I work. I could get there in under an hour, even, assuming that I stop at home first to change. Maybe Diane is right, after all.

I type back: *I haven't been but that sounds like a plan to me. It'll have to be around seven, though. Is that alright?*

Before I can even put my phone down, he texts back.

Great! Let's say... seven thirty?

My lips curl upward. *Awesome. See you there.*

There's a nervousness that's half excitement, half unease that stays with me for the rest of the workday. And why do I keep thinking about Charlie?

Jason is single. He's hot. And he wants commitment.

I don't look up again until Diane sticks her head over my cubicle, just before five twenty.

"Time to go! I was thinking that you should leave your car here, and I'll drive. I think I have something for you to wear, if it'll fit..." I cringe at Diane, realizing I never told her. *Shit.* I feel like an ass.

"Actually, I had a change of plans." I draw out the sentence to soften the blow then smile hopefully, "I'm going on a date tonight." My smile is wide, hoping she'll be happy for me. After all she's always talking about how I need to hookup and get laid.

Happy isn't exactly her response though. She looks a little shocked at first, and I feel awful. With the smile on my face vanished, I apologize "I should have told you when I got the message, but I was hung up on that a-hole client."

I always keep my plans with her and everyone else, chicks before dicks and all that, but one on one with Diane is hard to take. With Ann it's way easier. And I really do need to find someone serious... and/or freeze my eggs. I'm on borrowed time, and suddenly finding a husband is at the top of my to-do list.

"Fine," she snaps. "I expect the Kleinpeters ad on my desk tomorrow, though."

I would flinch at her sharp demeanor, but I'm used to it. She's also not my boss, she's just another designer on the job. "Already done. I cc'd you in the email."

"You sent an ad to the client without my approval?" she asks, her fury evident.

I grind my teeth slightly, wanting very much to remind her that she's not my fucking boss. "Correct. I don't have to get your approval. I was just doing it to be polite."

Her gaze narrows. "I don't know about that."

"Well, I do," I reply cheerfully, deciding I don't need this shit. "If you have a problem with it, I think HR is a good place to start."

She's practically shooting lasers out of her eyes now; it's almost comical. Diane has a long history of complaints filed against her in HR, mostly dress code violations. HR is the last place she would go for help.

"Have a great date," she says through clenched teeth and an expression that's reminiscent of sucking on a lemon.

"See you tomorrow!" I call out, feeling vindicated, but still uneasy. She can really be a bitch. I don't know why I put up with her as much as I do. Well other than the fact that I have no choice since I can't fire her.

Diane disappears, and I relax a little but that doesn't last long. I have a to do list that keeps growing, and more importantly, a date.

Chapter
FOUR

Charlie

Stretching my arms over my head I crack my back, feeling the exhaustion from working all last night until 5 am get to me. Damn the stretch feels good though. I couldn't sleep more than four hours with all the work that needed to be done before opening this afternoon for Mags. I need to hire someone new. Someone with experience who already knows what to do because I sure as hell don't have the time to train someone. *Needle*, meet *haystack.*

"Pass the gravy," Pops tells me. He's to my left, expecting me to pay attention when I can barely keep my eyes open.

After stifling a yawn, I reach across the table for the white ceramic rooster that holds the gravy. I'm fairly sure it's supposed to be for milk or creamer, but before I can take it my sister Cheryl bats my hand away.

"I'm not done with it," she tells me. I raise both my hands in surrender.

"Then pour it on your damn plate," Pops says, staring at the gravy. He's got a full plate of carved turkey, mashed potatoes and corn, with a fork in his right hand. He's acting like he's going to starve this minute if he doesn't get that gravy on, more than likely, every inch of his dinner.

"Language!" Ma snaps at him and I chuckle. She passes him the gravy though, and makes my sister gasp. That's what she gets for taking forever spooning out the potatoes I guess.

It's just the six of us tonight. Ali is at my left like usual, Ma's across from me and Pops is seated at the head of the table on my right. Ali's fiancé Michael sits on the end next to her while Cheryl sits across from her.

"I need the gravy, Ma," Cheryl says with a pout.

It's hard to imagine that Cheryl is a grown ass woman with a child from the way she just whined.

Cutting into my turkey and taking a bite, I don't wait for the gravy that's become such a commodity. I'm starving and I didn't realize it until I smelled dinner. Shit, I don't even remember the last time I ate. We were slammed today with both orders, and customers. Business is good, but I'm dog tired. Cheryl stifles a yawn as well as she looks over her shoulder at the rocker holding her sleeping baby. Rocker or swing, I don't know. Apparently there's a difference and Evie won't sleep in one of the contraptions. From what my brother-in-law says, the baby doesn't sleep at all.

"I need to eat fast," Cheryl says beneath her breath; maybe we were sharing the same thought. She rubs the sleep from her eyes with one hand, while spooning in corn with the other.

Ma places her elbows on the table, folding her hands for grace.

"Oh," Ali chirps up. "Can I say grace?"

I set my fork down although it clinks on the plate, drawing the attention of my entire family as I try to pretend I'm not chewing.

Family dinner. Every Sunday. No exception.

Except for the fact that today is Tuesday. Cheryl needed to get out of the house with Evie and Ma decided this dinner was mandatory.

Cheryl doesn't like being alone all day, every day, and I can't blame her. She's a social creature and being alone in the house with a newborn all day has got to be rough. Especially with the no sleeping part. Ma said it's family dinner tonight, so that's all there is to it.

"Wait for grace," my mother scolds me under her breath, giving Cheryl a pass which my widened eyes and darting glance points out.

"Can I say it?" Ali repeats, with even more desperation this time around.

I never wait for grace. Ma shakes her head at me and nods in response to Ali.

My youngest sister's excitement makes my lips kick up into a smirk. She grabs her napkin off of the table and smooths it out on her lap over her pale blue dress, all the while waiting for everyone to bow their heads.

"As long as it has nothing to do with the wedding," Michael says under his breath next to her. My grin widens as Alison's mouth opens in disbelief.

Pops chuckles to my right, and I can't help doing the same. Both Ma and Ali are obsessed over this wedding; it's all the women in this family ever talk about lately.

"Hush." Ma waves Michael away and bows her head. We all follow suit, the room quieting down as we wait.

"Bless us, Lord. Thank you for these gifts, which we are about to receive... Including my wedding," Ali says. She lifts her head to peek at Michael. He huffs a small laugh and shakes his head while resting his forehead on his hands. She pauses a minute, waiting for him to do or say anything, but he's quiet. "May you stay with us through our journey and bless us along the way. Amen."

The second she's done, the forks are lifted and the conversation continues. Michael and Pops are talking about the game last night. I'm half listening, half trying to eat as fast as I can so I can get back home.

"I can't believe Joseph had to work," Ma says... again.

She's brought it up about half a dozen times since I've been here. Ma has one wish, and it's for everyone to be home on Sunday. Joseph's a mechanic and owns his own shop. Usually it's not a problem, but he's been working more since little Evelyn came along.

"We need the extra money," Cheryl says softly. There are bags under her eyes, and I can tell she's just as tired as I am, maybe even more so. Pops motions for me to pass her the gravy, but Michael leans over the table and snatches it before I can. He's quick with it and then hands it off to Cheryl.

That white ceramic rooster brightens her spirits as Cheryl sits straighter in the chair and pours it all over the turkey and mashed potatoes. She's practically smothering her entire plate with the gravy.

Just before she sets it down, little Miss Evie starts crying for the first time since she's been here. Cheryl's head whips around, and her face falls.

"No, no, no," she says quietly. She walks over and shushes Evie softly while rocking the bassinet. She's fucking exhausted.

"She's still not sleeping well?" Ali asks while craning her neck to see the baby.

Cheryl presses her lips into a thin line and shakes her head. Her expression has completely fallen.

"I'll take her," I speak without thinking and scoot my chair out some, the legs scraping on the wooden floor and hold my hands out. Cheryl doesn't waste a second to round the table with the little two-month-old all bundled up in her arms.

"Thank you," she says quickly, ready to eat her dinner like it's a race.

I've got a soft spot for Evie. She's the first baby I've ever held and to be honest I didn't know if I was doing it right. Her eyes are closed, and her hands are balled into little fists as Cheryl settles her on my chest. She's so small, such a tiny little thing with hardly any weight to her. She knows how to scream though, that's for certain.

I shush her and pat her bottom rhythmically as Cheryl takes off back to her seat and doesn't even scoot in before grabbing her fork.

My entire body moves slightly as I bounce little Evie, trying to get her to calm down. Her cry isn't loud like it was a moment ago and it doesn't affect me in the least, but I know it'll calm Cheryl down again if Evie is happy. It only takes a moment before Evie lays her head on my chest and lets out a long yawn. I watch her face as she falls back asleep and I slowly stop bouncing her.

"Oh, that's so cute," Ali squeals before shoveling a mouthful of potatoes in.

"Aw, it is. My oldest boy." Ma sounds so proud, but I completely avoid her gaze. I know what's coming next, and it's only when she says the words that I regret offering to hold Evie.

"You need one of your own, I think," Ma says matter-of-factly. She grabs the gravy and puts a modest amount over her turkey. I believe the rooster has made its way to everyone but me.

I have to readjust Evie slightly so I can hold her against my chest with only my left arm.

I ignore Ma and say, "It's 'cause I'm a heater. Puts her right to sleep."

With my right hand free, I cut the turkey with my fork and take another bite.

"You do need one," Cheryl says. I practically choke on the turkey. I stare at her down the table, feeling like she just stabbed me in the back.

"Babies are so wonderful," she says softly. I don't even know how to respond she's obviously deranged from lack of sleep.

"I'd need a wife for that. And I'm fine with the current state when it comes to that." I grip my glass on the table and take a quick swig, feeling my body tense up before I set the glass down.

I keep my eyes on my plate, ignoring everyone else. We've had this conversation so many times. Over and over, for five long years. Both my sisters are younger, both moving on with their lives the way they should according to this small town.

My plans got fucked over. Literally. And Ma never fails to remind me that I need to get back on track.

"You know I saw Susanne's mother the other day—"

I cut my mother off, feeling the frustration of just wanting to eat a damn meal in this house without talking about that woman.

"I'd rather not talk about it or her." I look her square in the eyes when I say it, and I know Ma immediately regrets bringing her up. I set my fork down and start rocking Evie again as her tummy grumbles.

It's not that she wants us to get back together. I know that. It's that my mother wants me to be happy again, like I was with Susanne. Or the way she thinks I was with her.

Ma has no idea.

This town has a good memory. Susanne and I were supposed to be just like Cheryl and Joseph. High school sweethearts, together through college, married by twenty-five and a baby not long after.

At thirty years old, with no plans of marriage, I'm failing those expectations.

But that's what happens when your fiancée and your best friend decide they should have a drunken weekend fling at the beach.

Everyone knows what they did, but no one talks about it. Not my family, and not most of the town. It's why I moved to the outskirts and bought the damn bar. Five years later, and the pain of her cheating on me is mostly gone. I'm numb. But I'm not fucking stupid. Both of them can go to hell.

Not all women cheat. I know that, and I'm over it. I don't feel like having my heart ripped out again. No fucking thank you. It's been five years since I took that ring back and showed Susanne the door… and kicked Adam's ass.

For a second, just a split second, I see Grace in my mind. I picture her absently checking her phone with that sad look on her face. She would never cheat. She knows what she wants. Suzanne wasn't sure. That's what she told me. I was all she ever had and so she needed to be sure.

I close my eyes as I shush Evie, forcing that conversation out of my head, my lips close to her head and my right hand patting her back. I know Grace has gotta be hurting about not being able to have kids. She's talked about it more than once to me. I don't like seeing that sadness behind those beautiful doe eyes of hers. She doesn't strike me as a woman who'd cheat. A woman like her isn't interested in a man like me though. She wants a commitment and a man with stability, and there's no way I'm getting her without promising her just that in return.

I've made too many mistakes, been burned too many times. The bar does great some weeks, not so great the next. She doesn't want me. She'd make cute little babies though.

Evie starts crying a little harder the second my bouncing stops. *Crap.* Cheryl hops up from her seat with her arms out ready to take her. I don't fight her in the least and pass Evie back to her.

I'm not ready for a relationship, let alone to be a father.

Chapter
FIVE

Grace

I've realized my nervous habit is tapping my foot, mainly because I keep catching myself doing it in between sips of white wine as I sit at the bar of The Brick Store Pub, waiting for my date to arrive. All around me, there are people in motion; waiters carrying trays of beer and food out to the tables, customers heading to the bathroom or upstairs to the Belgian beer bar with the chefs peeking their heads out of the back to check out the crowd.

With stylish deep-red sailor pants and a cream-colored blouse, I really tried to look cute. I debated on keeping the third button undone to add a little bit of sexy but opted to keep it modest. After another sip of Zinfandel, I suck my teeth, a habit that reappears when I feel like I'm at a disadvantage. I haven't dated in how long?

At least I made it on time.

It's 7:48, exactly eighteen minutes past when Jason and I agreed to meet. I'm officially nervous now and I keep checking my phone to see if he's messaged. I'm sure it's just traffic. I drum my fingers against the arched bar top, shaped like a large horseshoe and stop myself from tapping my foot again. The red stilettos are too pretty to ding up over a date that never happened. I contemplate ordering a second glass after finishing the wine... or maybe a drink I've been eyeing since I've been here for something like twenty-seven minutes. Not that I'm counting.

Right as I'm about to wave to the bartender, my hand rising, Jason appears. I do a double take while he grins at me. His eyes are level with mine, and I'm five foot four. There's no way he's six feet tall, as it says on his dating profile.

He's also paunchy and balding a little. His photos must have been REALLY old, like they were probably taken in college.

He's still cute though. I remind myself and force any hint of my thoughts off my face. Those pictures did not prepare me though.

Deep breaths. We're doing this!

I swallow and extend my hand to him as he walks up, reminding myself that looks aren't everything. *Even though my photos are recent.*

"Hi. I'm Grace," I say, managing a smile although my mouth feels dry. Oh my goodness my heart is racing with nerves out of nowhere.

"Hey," he says, ignoring my offer of a handshake. Instead, he crushes me to his body, hugging me forcefully. *Oh, he's a hugger.* My inner voice sounds as shocked as I feel. The nervous laugh that leaves me probably gives that away. When he pulls back, his hands still on my shoulders, I'm a little out of breath. "I'm Jason," he says with a grin, patting my shoulders before finally releasing me.

He's wearing khaki shorts and a blue button-up, with fancy sunglasses peeking out of the pocket. He tosses his car keys on the bar, making sure the Porsche insignia is visible. From the look on his face to the air around him, this guy is *cocky*. I'm so shocked that my mouth is even hanging open a little, but I honestly can't help it.

Alarm bells are going off in my head, telling me to get out, right now. He is nothing like the person I've been talking to.

"How about a drink?" Jason suggests. I could use about a dozen right now to settle down, but my legs feel like Jell-O.

I picture Charlie, my stool, a cool glass of something he whipped up for me.

Oh, my gosh, I blink away my crazy. Pining after Charlie is literally insane.

"Um, okay," I say, reaching for the menu so I can order the special I wanted and pretend like I'm not hung up on someone so unavailable.

"No no," he says playfully. "I'll pick something you'll love. I'm kind of a craft beer aficionado." He grabs the menu, taking a seat at the bar before turning back to me with a charming smile and saying, "And I'm really good at guessing what people like."

"Oh. Well okay."

I try to talk myself out of the obnoxious first impression I got, after all, Charlie makes me surprise drinks all the time. And there I go again... *what is wrong with me?*

The drink I was eyeing up was something called a Burial Shadow Clock, but maybe he'll know that. Or maybe he'll introduce me to something I didn't know I liked. That thought eases me and I find myself smiling. I take another peek at Jason but find myself comparing his smooth jaw to Charlie's stubbled one and suddenly I need that drink right this second.

I let out a bit of the tension in my body and take a seat next to him. Staying positive is my main goal. Jason's not quite how I thought he'd be, but I'm sure the same is true for him.

He skims the menu, then calls the bartender over, ordering two stouts. The bartender asks him whether it'll be cash or card, and Jason looks to me.

"What'll it be?" he asks.

"Oh! Uhh... Visa, please." My cheeks heat with embarrassment.

I turn and get my wallet from my purse, fumbling to get my credit card to start a tab. I already paid for the first glass and stare at the empty glass, wishing it was full again. The tight smile stays on my face as I hand it to the same bartender as before. It's only when the man side-eyes Jason that I realize he's not reaching for his card. Jason taps his hands on the bar top and looks past the bartender to the television screens behind him.

The bartender gives me a dubious look, then goes to run the card. Shake off the unease. It's fine. I'll get the drinks and I bet he'll get dinner. Maybe that's the way it works normally? Or maybe... maybe he's thinking something else, I don't know.

Shifting uncomfortably on the stool, I try to shake it off. I'm a little more than put out that Jason assumed I could pay for his beer as I watch the bartender pour it, but unsure how to say so. I glance at him, biting down on my lip, and he smirks.

"I like to let the woman pick up the first tab," he says. "Not that I can't buy a drink. It's just, you know, figure out if they're gold diggers, you know?"

Gold digger? One drink. No dinner with this guy unless things change around tremendously. Making myself that promise I glance between the second pint the bartender is filling and my date.

Jason stares at me expectantly, like he really wants a response to his comment. My lips curl down into a partial frown as I offer, "We could have split the check."

"Yeah, but I want a woman who earns, you know what I mean? A woman who knows how to be aggressive about what she wants."

I'm a little flabbergasted at that, and I know it shows on my face. Luckily the bartender shows up at that moment, setting two dark beers down in front of us.

This has got to be new-date-jitters. I couldn't have been so wrong about this guy.

"Oh," I say, looking at the beer's dark chocolate color. It reminds me a bit of chocolate milk for some reason. I don't normally drink beer, but when I do, I'm a pale ale kind of girl. Feeling my stress level climb higher and higher, I purse my lips a little and wonder what I'm doing here.

"What's wrong?" Jason asks, drawing my attention to him.

Oh so much is wrong, but I stick with the polite answer, "I don't usually care for dark beer much, but I'm excited to give it a try." A small smile slips onto my face when he grins at my statement.

"You will," he nods, picking up his pint glass for a toast. "What should we toast to?"

"How about to new experiences?"

"No, no," he corrects me. "To us."

He clinks his glass against mine, and it spills a tiny bit of the beer over my hand onto the bar top. I can practically hear him guzzling still after I take a sip of the beer, ignoring the spilled beer and simply laughing it off. Two small square napkins is enough to clean it up anyway. The bitter taste in my mouth sits on my tongue. Yup, nope, I don't like dark beer.

Sitting easily on the stool as I take another sip of the beer. It's indeed like chocolate milk… if chocolate milk is rancid and bitter.

I take yet another sip, thinking that maybe I just need to close my eyes and let it wash over my tongue…

Nope. I sit my beer down and push it away, relegating it to the far edge of the bar.

"Not to your liking?" Jason asks.

"Not so much," I say, reaching for the menu. "You can have it if you want?"

Jason grabs the menu again before I can get to it. "Let me choose again."

Railroaded isn't something I'm used to feeling, but that's exactly how I feel now and I can't help the frown that I know is revealed in my expression.

I stare at this man and I don't know what to do. I'm not used to being such a shrew on dates, not that I've really been on many, but that's exactly how I feel. Then again I've never been treated like this. My lips part to say as much, but he's already waving the bartender down and ordering another beer.

"I like Belgian wheat beers, if that helps," I say to the bartender, as soon as Jason's done talking. I didn't even listen to what he said.

"Just bring her what I asked for," Jason says pointedly.

The bartender senses the tension between me and Jason,

so he just backs off and pours another beer. On my tab, I presume.

"So, first date formalities," Jason says, as though none of that ever happened.

I have been on so many shitty dates in college. They didn't really matter though as I wasn't actually looking for a forever Mr. Right. Just a Mr. Right now. I watch Jason as he talks and realize this one is probably the worst start to any interaction with any individual I've ever had. Including some of my worst clients. *Probably.*

"Let's see... I'm in finance, but I won't even begin to explain it. It's nothing you would understand. I'm from Atlanta, but left for college and then came back." Jason doesn't look at me as he recites what's probably a rehearsed introduction, motioning with his hands in between drinking the beer. "I went to Westminster, of course. Followed by Columbia and Yale, for business school. Came back to help my father run his firm. I've been everywhere. You name it, I've been there. I spend my weekends on my boat. And you?"

He finally looks up at me. I take a breath, my fingers tangling in my lap. Everywhere? He's been everywhere? Irritation claws at me.

"Well... I'm from Atlanta, too. I went to Decatur High School—"

"A public school?" he interrupts.

I wait a moment to answer him, my body heat rising. "Yes. I also went to Brenau University—"

"You went where?" he asks, his nose wrinkling.

"Brenau? It's a women's college—"

"Oh, a *girls* school," he says, tapping his hand on the bar top and leaning back some on his stool. I smile thinly.

"It's actually a private college." It's where I went before

Rhode Island School of Design. Both are damn good institutions, and I'm proud of the fact I was accepted to them.

He actually rolls his eyes as he takes another drink of the beer, the one I paid for, and says, "Yeah, okay."

I seriously need to get out of here.

He takes a moment to savor his beer. I stand, shouldering my purse. Anger is just simmering beneath the surface. I've never been treated so poorly in my life.

"Where are you going?" he asks, surprised.

"I'm going to go ahead and leave," I say.

"Wait—you can't just leave like this, in the middle of our date!" He has the nerve to raise his voice loud enough to get the attention of the men around us.

I wave my arm frantically at the bartender, not because he doesn't see but more than likely because of the nerves racing through me. "I'd like to close out."

A night with Diane would have actually been better than this.

The bartender must see my frustration from where he's pouring drinks down the bar because he says, "You're all set, it's on the house."

"Thanks!" I call to him and wish it came out less shaky. He's literally my hero right now for not making me wait another second with the jackass who has already turned his back to me to ask a woman a few seats down if she wants a drink he just paid for.

I don't even bother to correct him; he isn't getting another second from me.

Rushing to get inside my car, I pull out of the parking lot, feeling completely sick over what just happened. Did that even happen? That was real, wasn't it?

Disbelief consumes me as I blow out a breath and my car

hits the interstate. I'm almost on autopilot driving through evening traffic while my mind is elsewhere, trying to forget what a miserable first date that was. I settle into my seat and try to calm down as I look at the time on the dashboard.

I don't want to go home and be alone after that bullshit. I know there's only one place I want to be right now, and only one guy's smile I want to see...

Chapter
SIX

Charlie

I found the perfect woman for you.
    She's going to be at the wedding.
        Leaning forward on the bar with my head in my hands, I groan when I read my mother's texts. I wish she'd just leave it alone. I don't have the time, or the energy. I'm not ready for anything serious. She's already text me twice since I left my parent's house to come back to work.

"Well." The barstool on the other side of the bar squeaks as she continues. "You look like you're having an even worse day than I am."

Grace's soft voice makes a grin play on my lips. I raise my head slowly, still resting my forearms on the bar, and peek up to see the pretty blue eyes I knew would be there staring back at me.

"You have no idea," I tell her as I push off the bar and stop mid response to my mother.

Grace turns her shoulder to me, the smell of her perfume wafting toward me. Her long hair falls off her shoulder and exposes more of the bare skin of her slender neck. All I can hear is the rustling in her purse while she looks for her card. This place is packed, but seeing her after the dinner I had tonight… it's like no one else is here.

A small huff of a laugh comes from deep in my throat. Grace has a few habits, and one of them is that she always puts her tab on her card when she's ordering food.

"The special?" I ask her. I walk backward toward the double doors that lead to the back.

She looks up at me, still hunched over her purse and smiles wide. "Of course."

Chicken tenders and fries. It's our special on Tuesdays, and Grace always gets the special. I call out to the back, pushing the doors open, then I grab her card to put the order through.

"What'll you have to drink, sweetheart?" I ask, looking up at her from across the bar. I have to raise my voice, and I see a few of the men look over at me and notice her.

They're regulars, and they go back to their food and drinks in no time, but I still feel a subtle rise of emotion. I don't know what the emotion is, but I ignore it when she answers that she'll have a pale ale.

"You got it." I move to the bottled beers. She likes the lighter variety with a bit of citrus. One night she went through nearly every pale ale on a mission to find her favorite. The cap pops off, and I toss it into the trash before handing her the cool bottle.

"You want a glass?" I offer even though I'm sure she doesn't.

Shaking her head, she answers "Nope," and reaches for the beer. Her fingers brush against my hand, and a shock goes through me. A heated current, lights my blood aflame. There's no reason for it. It was only the barest of touches, but holy hell the sparks were there.

A violent blush heats her face and I wonder if she felt it, too. I wait a second as she clears her throat and looks away, shier than normal, despite being dressed to the nines in some sexy outfit I've never seen before, some dark red pants and a light cream blouse.

"Charlie!" I almost flinch at the sound of my name, snapping me back to the present. Frankie calls my name from down the bar. He's at the very end, but he didn't have to yell so damn loud.

"Yeah?" I have to turn away from Grace to stride toward him, which is probably good all things considered with how she looked away when our fingers touched. My skin feels hotter with every second that passes. I want to turn around and I can feel her gorgeous eyes on me, willing me to look at her.

"One more?" he asks me, rather than tells me.

I lean against the bar and shrug. "Whatever you want."

He nods as he pushes his empty beer bottle toward me. It takes me less than a minute to get him another drink.

The back doors creaks behind me, signifying Maggie coming out of the back, letting the one double door swing open and shut carelessly as she balances Grace's order in her hands.

I'm quick to grab the plate with both hands to help Maggie out.

"I got it," I tell her even as the skeptical look hits her eyes and tilted brow. Maggie wipes both of her hands on her apron and nods, the look not leaving her even as she leaves me to go back to the kitchen.

The smell of the fries and chicken and bacon wakes me

right the fuck up. I'm still full from dinner, but I'm definitely going to snag a few fries from Grace.

A smile crosses my lips as I set the plate down in front of her, remembering the first time she ordered the Tuesday special. She practically threatened me if I didn't eat a few fries with her.

It was the second night she came in here. I remember the first because she came with a friend. She's almost Grace's opposite. I remember thinking it didn't make sense that the two of them would be friends. There was a third one with them, but she left early. Leaving the loud blonde and an embarrassed Grace.

The next night, Grace came back alone, and I have to admit I was curious about her. She must've overheard me tell someone I hadn't eaten dinner yet.

That happens a lot when you're managing so much. Time just slips by.

She called me over and said it was too much food for her. I politely declined, but she wasn't having it. This sweet little thing told me I had to eat, and she'd tell my manager on me if I didn't. I don't think I've ever smiled so wide before.

She really is a sweetheart.

"So you're having a bad day?" I ask her. I pull my barstool over to her, grateful to sit down and think about something other than work and my mother's text. If she's not here by 6 maybe 6:30, I assume she's not coming by. Sometimes she surprises me with a later arrival, like tonight. She's here a little earlier than the rush and thankfully James actually came in tonight. I've got time and now a spare man for tonight. There was no way I was going to put him on the schedule without having back up in case he didn't show. I told him there's a three strike system now, he's already got one down. He'll either shape up, or ship out.

Grace rolls her eyes before grabbing a chicken tender. As she starts to talk, I realize I forgot the salt. That woman likes her salt.

"So I went out on a date tonight." She lets out a heavy sigh as I leave her for all of three seconds to grab the salt and pepper, even though she won't use it, and I feel my jaw clench a little tighter at the word, 'date.'

The barstool tilts on two legs as I reach over and grab the one bottle of ketchup on this half of the bar and set it down in front of her.

"Thank you," she says politely. She always covers her chicken tenders with salt. No ketchup, they're for the fries. No barbeque sauce. Just a little salt.

"Oh yeah, a date? And who is this Prince Charming?" I'm surprised by the jealousy I feel as I look back at her gorgeous eyes while she cocks a brow as if to say, 'you have no reason to be jealous.'

"It was awful," she says comically and a genuine smile graces her lips as she lets out a huff of a feminine laugh. A wave of relief washes over me. Holding onto the edge of the barstool and spreading my legs a little wider, I listen to her tell me about this guy, Jason.

I steal a fry, and then another. Each time it only makes her smile more. After a few fries remind me how full I am from dinner I know I'm not really hungry, but I'm used to stealing a bit off her plate when she orders food. I guess we both have some habits now.

"And then what?" I ask her wanting to know more about this horrible date.

I wonder what it was like from his perspective. If he really saw her for who she is. The thought makes my heart do a small flip, but I barely notice as her hand absently brushes mine again and she leans in. The sparks are still there, but I'm better at hiding that it happened this time around.

"I can't even tell you," she states and she's animated as she talks. "It was just something about him. He was so… so… arrogant and cocky. He was rude." She purses her lips for a minute. "And he was definitely balding."

Letting out a chuckle, I take in the bar with a smile. The floor's covered, patrons are being served and Frankie's going to need another in about five minutes.

My phone rings and I absently check it, forgetting that I was in the middle of a conversation with Ma before Grace came in.

I know you got the text, Charlie. I'm only trying to help.

Deleting what I was going to send before, I text my mom back: *I know Ma. Love you* and hit the side button on my phone, pushing off of the bar to get myself a water. I could really use a beer, but I learned a long time ago not to let that happen on the clock. I have to set an example. If you're working, you're not drinking.

"What's wrong?" Grace asks. I grab a bottle of water from the built-in beverage refrigerator.

I don't answer her right away. Instead, I twist the cap off and take a swig and then another. I should really grab a Coke; I need the caffeine. Giving her a one armed shrug, I set the bottle down below the counter and make my way back to the stool in front of Grace. My eyes travel to the clock on the side wall. It's going to get busy real soon.

"It's nothing. Just my mom checking in on me," I say.

Grace's expression doesn't give much away, but she keeps looking at me. She cocks a brow, pressing me for more information.

An easy laugh rumbles up through my chest as I grab the

bottle and take another sip. "My sister's getting married, and my ma thinks she's going to set me up at the wedding."

Grace must get a real good kick out of that, judging by the huge smile on her face. I never noticed how perfect her smile is. Damn, those doe eyes light right up, too. They're shining with happiness as she claps her hands once and smiles.

"You think, it's funny that she's trying to hook me up with someone?" I tease her. "Better than OKCupid or whatever you're using."

Her eyebrows raise, and she purses her lips before taking another french fry and biting into it. She wags the half of fry left at me before admitting, "You're probably right."

It's quiet for a moment, and my phone pings again.

We both look at it on the bar, but I don't flip it over to see what Ma said. It's probably just 'I love you too'.

"You should probably answer her," Grace says with a sly smile.

I steal two fries and shove them into my mouth, staring at her the whole time.

She gapes at me. She looks at the phone as if she's going to take it, but she doesn't. I like this more aggressive, competitive side of her.

She doesn't push though, instead she takes a sip of her beer.

I reach for my phone, giving in and I don't miss the smile on Grace's face as she takes another sip of her beer. There are actually two messages waiting for me:

I love you too. But seriously... She's really nice, and available!

You should meet the girl Ma's talking about.

That second one is from Ali. I toss the phone down onto

the bar and let out a frustrated sigh. I know they're only play-ing, and they're only trying to help, but I'm not interested. A light goes off in my head, and I finally pick up the phone and type a response.

I'm already seeing someone. So I don't need a date.

Not thirty seconds after setting the phone down does it go off over and over.

What?

Who?

When were you going to tell me about it?

Is she coming to the wedding?

"Oh my God." Grace's eyes go wide, although she can't contain the wide grin on her face. "What did you tell her?"

Sitting up straighter on her stool, she leans over to look as another few text messages come in.

I watch her reaction as she scrolls through them deli-cately, just using her pointer finger and leaving the phone sit-ting on the bar. I'm taken aback when the smile falls from her face and she slowly sits back on her stool.

Why didn't you tell me?

I don't believe you…

Bring the girl to the wedding, or else!

"So you have a girlfriend?" she asks me softly. I'm not sure if I'm imagining the hurt there, or if it's genuine.

I grab the phone and read the messages again as I answer. "No, no girlfriend."

"So you lied?" The happiness comes right back as she bites down on her bottom lip, her eyes on me.

I let a small chuckle slip out. "Yeah. But now I'm screwed."

"Just say she can't come." Grace shrugs, grabbing a fry and chewing at the end. She has no idea what how adamant my family will be to meet this *new girlfriend*. I can't for the life of me think what I was doing. Maybe I'm just sleep deprived.

After grabbing Frank a beer and asking a few guests if they need anything, I head back to Grace with the inevitable truth: "They're going to want proof."

"What?" she says like they're crazy.

"You didn't grow up in a small town, did you?" I ask her. She has no idea what it's like. When everyone knows everything, and word gets around faster than a forest fire in a drought.

She shakes her head, finishing off the fry and reaching for one of the last remaining fried pieces of deliciousness.

"I grew up in Ellijay. My family is nosy, but so is the whole town. Everybody knows everybody's business." I pause, considering. "I shouldn't have told them I'm seeing someone."

Grace sucks on the tips of her two fingers quickly, most likely for that last bit of salt, and my eyes are drawn to her mouth. She doesn't mean it to be sexual as she licks the salt clean, but I'll be damned if it doesn't turn me on.

"Take a picture of us," she offers with a nonchalant shoulder lift. "I'll pretend to be your girlfriend for the picture and there's your proof."

She winks at me and grabs her beer, although that beautiful blush comes back with a vengeance.

It feels like a dare, and I'm happy to take it. I reach for the phone and scoot closer to her. Smiling, I snap a couple of photos.

As I sit back down on my seat I take a look at them; one is just right. She's drinking her beer, although she's smiling still. She looks sweet, happy even. I think Ma would like her.

"That'll get them off your back," Grace says. There's that same dare hidden in her voice, but the effect is dimmed as she looks away and bites down on her bottom lip. *My shy sweetheart.*

As I hit send, Grace finishes off her beer. I don't hesitate to get her another. I know she wants it.

This time when our fingers touch, I don't let the bottle go. She tugs a bit harder, then realizes I'm messing with her. The smile lights up her face and the texts light up my phone on the bar.

Grace grabs it before I can, letting go of the beer.

Her mouth forms a beautiful "O" as she gapes at the screen. I can only imagine her lips wrapped around my cock like that. I shamefully adjust my hardening dick in my jeans as she points to the phone, completely unaware. Damn I want this chick. How have I not wanted her this bad before tonight?

"They really want me to come to the wedding," she teases and her sweet laugh is music to my ears.

"It's two weeks away," I say and then take a sip of her beer. I shouldn't, but it's only one sip. And it's hers. "You really want to play my girlfriend for two weeks and go to the wedding with me?"

I ask the question playfully, but there's a serious hint hidden in there. *A dare.*

"What do I get?" she asks.

"What do you want?" My dick twitches in my pants at the thought of her answering with that desire I see in her eyes.

"Let me think about what I want," she answers in a soft voice.

She grabs the second to last fry and watches as I slowly reach the last one.

"What is it that you get again? You're willing to do

something for just a date?" she asks, forcing my eyes to reach hers.

"Nope. It's more than just a date. It's my family off my back."

I nod to the phone and bite the fry as I wait for her response. *Tell me what you want, sweetheart. I'll give it to you.*

"Okay then... you've got yourself a deal."

"What's my end of the bargain?" I ask her with a smirk on my face.

She bites down on her bottom lip and I know what she wants is right there, on the tip of her tongue, but she won't say it. I know what she wants. She wants to go slumming, get all tangled up in the sheets with the man she thinks I am. All she has to do is ask. Hell, she can have me every night for these two weeks and then some.

"I'll figure something out," she says, shifting on her barstool.

I'm playing with fire, knowing damn well this girl wants to settle down. She doesn't want to wind up with me, I know that much. But I'll play along.

This is all for fun. I just need to remember that. It's just a drunken deal; it probably won't even happen.

Chapter
SEVEN

Grace

I want you to knock me up.

I could feel the words on the tip of my tongue when I was making a deal with Charlie, even though I know that's not realistic and sounds absolutely insane.

1. It's not an even trade.
2. A baby isn't a decision to make in a bar with a kind-of-friend.
3. I have officially lost my mind.

I'll figure out how I'm going to deal with my… issues. But for now, I'm focusing on the positive. I have a date… sort of. It's just pretend but… yeah, I'm going to treat it like a date because dammit I want a nice date and a refresher on exactly how to date.

As I drive home from Mac's, I can't help the smile that lights up my face. It's silly, I know. The very idea of Charlie going on a date with me is laughable. I get that.

But I still let my imagination run wild as I drive back into the city.

Fantasies about Charlie picking me up for the wedding run through my head and I just laugh it off. I'd wear a pretty pale blue dress, lacy but not scandalous, and dark blue heels. A giddy squeal leaves me when I imagine opening the front door to my apartment, and he takes a moment to look at me. *Really* look at me, and drink me in.

Standing there in his wedding tux, I assume… since he's probably a groomsman, he looks fucking dashing. In the fantasy, I bite my lip and look downward, trying not to show him all the emotions just beneath the surface.

He whistles, long and low. My eyes drift up, catching his.

"Damn, you *are* the kind of girl I'd like to date," he says. "As a matter of fact, I think you'd look even better if you were carrying my child…"

I can't help but laugh out loud in my car as I pull into my parking spot. My reverie fizzles away, gone like smoke. *How ridiculous!*

Okay, so the real Charlie definitely wouldn't say that and that's not how this is going to go down, but I'd rather think of that than my nearly-forgotten, crap date from tonight. My cheeks hurt from smiling as I turn the car off and shake my head. I need to get my head on straight, because going to Charlie's sister's wedding isn't even a *real* date. I'm probably not even on his radar, for God's sake. It's just meaningless flirting. For all I know, he's not actually going to go through with this plan.

Yeah it's definitely not going to happen and that's just fine. It's fun to daydream though. So long as my silly little heart keeps itself in check. Charlie is a friend and nothing else.

Sighing as I get out of my car, I lock up the idea at the

same time as I lock up my car and then climb the two flights of stairs to my apartment. Only on the tenth stair do I feel the weight of the drinks I've had. I'm not too tipsy but I am more tired than I realized. I usually don't stay out this long, but tonight, I didn't want to leave.

It's quiet out tonight, the city lulled to sleep by a long day of constant rushing.

The breeze feels nice tonight too. The keys jingle as I toss them in the bowl on the front entry table next to my purse.

Illuminating my tiny studio with a flick of the switch, I take it all in with new eyes, as Charlie would see it for the first time. Once upon a time, I found the fact that my bed overlooks the fire escape romantic. I used to like the way that my kitchen is just a small bar, with a mini fridge and stove.

I used to be charmed by the tiny bathroom, painted in a soft shade of purple with retro white tile. Back when I found this place, I was glad that I had something in the big city that I could call my own.

The mattress groans as I sit down on the frilly white bed and take my shoes off. I kick them over to the wall where I have my 'closet,' i.e. a hanging rack jammed full and ready to tip over. I rub the sleep from my eyes and then take a good look around at the space I spent so much time making mine.

I know I have to move soon. I've lived here for almost four years, and it was great in college and the couple of years after. But now I have a real job and I'm doing well, so...

I need to seriously think about moving.

The weight of the day hits me as I undress and then crawl into bed, wondering where I should move to. Climbing under the comforter the answer is obvious to me and the neighborhood around Mac's flashes in my mind. There are plenty of cute houses for rent in Vinings.

A blush flames my cheeks when I realize that I'm actually fantasizing about living near Charlie, but it's not like I didn't think about living there before I ever set eyes on the man. I settle on my side, staring out the window to the fire escape.

I imagine living close enough to Charlie that he just *stops by* late at night, his broad shoulders and quiet grin filling my doorway. I groan aloud, turning onto my back.

Charlie, Charlie, Charlie… I have a one-track mind today.

His sister's wedding is *not* a date! I need to remember that, to get it through my thick skull.

He just asked me to pacify his family and not get set up on a blind date. As I stare at the ceiling, I honestly can't believe that he asked me, or that I said yes. But after he sent the picture of us together to his mom, it was kinda hard to say no. I definitely blame it on the alcohol, and on the smile that Charlie pinned me with.

The combination of those two things is enough to get any girl to drop her guard.

I've been a regular at Mac's for long enough that if he was into me, he would have already asked me out before now. And it wouldn't be some stupid deal to keep his family off his back.

The worries and anxiety attached to IVF and knowing I should freeze my eggs come back and hit me like a ton of bricks… or maybe like walking straight into a cold shower. I haven't even considered that I'll need a bigger place to live if I do get pregnant. A new house with separate rooms, that could accommodate a nursery, unlike my studio.

I'm so ready to be a parent in my heart of hearts, but so not ready on a practical level. There's so much that will have to change before I can have a child.

A strangled noise of frustration climbs up my throat, and I jump up to get my cell phone from my purse. *How did I forget to charge it?* Getting back in bed, I open the Tinder dating app, the long cord from the charger reaching to the middle of the bed just fine.

I purse my lips as I swipe through several guys. I swipe left for pass, right for potential. I swipe left several times, stopping on a hot guy. Dark hair, tan, tallish from his pictures…

But I see that he's just visiting Atlanta from Texas this weekend. I swipe left regretfully, turning him down. There are half a dozen of the same kind of men, a hot guy just looking for a girl to show him the city for the weekend.

Not for me, unfortunately. I swipe for a couple more minutes, then Tinder lets me know I'm out of matches. I surrender and pretend I didn't just do that to convince myself I'm not hung up on Charlie and any potential there. Heck, I don't even have his phone number.

Maybe it's crazy to think that I can get a baby and the man of my dreams from one person. Maybe I get the hottie later —after I have a baby on my own.

I picture myself with a grinning baby in my arms, both of us beyond happy. I don't really *need* a guy to give me that, do I? Maybe freezing my eggs waiting for the man isn't the way to go.

Of course, getting a donor from a sperm bank is pricey and clinical. I've never even considered it an option, but the more I think about it…

My eyes wander back to my phone. I could get a donor myself, the old-fashioned way. Hook up with some super hot, super smart guy without protection. A guy like Charlie.

Biting my lip, I know that's sooooo wrong.

1. I'd have to tell him.
2. I definitely wouldn't be his pretend date then because… yeah, no way. No way would that work.

A small piece of me wonders, if I just asked him, would he say yes?

He's hotter than fire, smart and runs his own business. Plus, Charlie wouldn't ask that many questions about a baby, right? Maybe he'd do it in exchange for me helping him out? *It's crazy.* I'm sure he'd think I was a fucking lunatic.

I'm sure there's a consent form or legal... thing.

Oh my God, I'm literally losing it. Pulling my covers around myself I huff out, "I have officially gone off the deep end," to no one. Further validating the fact that I have lost my mind.

Chapter
EIGHT

Charlie

"Don't you ever sleep?" Maggie's voice rings out from the back room.

Looking over my shoulder to spot her and her bright yellow tee sporting a beer company on the front, I set the box of craft beers, same brand, on the floor in the stockroom. It's a local company a friend of Mags started a couple of years ago. Damn good, too. The bottles rattle slightly as I stand up, stretching my back.

"Morning," I tell her, stifling my yawn. My shift last night ended around three in the morning, but the food trucks will be here first thing. Going through inventory was more important than sleep apparently.

Maggie sets her purse down on the long bench just outside my office door. The kitchen and storage are in one area, and my office is all the way in the back. It's not the best setup, but it works.

There are so many things I'd change if I could. One day. Little by little I get it all done. A grateful sigh leaves me as I crack my neck and I walk past her to grab my coffee. I can't believe it's eight already. I need to get home, get into my bed and actually sleep. But first, coffee. Black with a hell of a lot of sugar.

The thought of sleeping, and burying my head in a pillow forces another yawn to creep up on me, and I cover my mouth, looking at the back door that leads to the parking lot and therefore my car before bringing the mug of coffee to my lips. It's lukewarm now, a little cold even. I drink it anyway. I'm used to having caffeine however I can get it at this point.

"Good morning to you, too," Maggie says with a tone that matches the worried look on her face. I ignore it. Maggie's always worried about something. If it's not me, it's someone else.

"You good to get the food prepped when the trucks come?" I ask as I walk across the kitchen to the sink. "James should be here for the heavy lifting and I'll wait for him to come in before leaving it all to you." She's done this before and I trust her more than anyone to do it right.

I rinse the mug out before setting it into the dishwasher and when she doesn't respond I know she's waiting for me to turn off the faucet and face her. Which is just what I do. Leaning against the sink makes me feel that much more tired.

"I am. And you didn't have to do this," she says as she gestures outward.

I shrug. Throwing the dish towel back down, I push off the sink. There are a number of issues I have, I know as much because my sister and Mags are real good at pointing them out. One of them is that I don't like handing off responsibility. It matters too much. This bar is what I have. It's all I have.

"You have control issues," Maggie tells me. Okay, so I have

the bar and control issues. I'm fine with those two. She checks one of the boxes closer to her, peeking in and nodding before she crosses her arms across her chest.

"What else am I gonna do other than keep my baby in shape?" I ask. I'm trying to be lighthearted, but the question makes my stomach sink.

I've got no one waiting for me at home and nothing to do besides run the bar. It never used to get to me, but the thought is making me second-guess everything as I close up the box she just opened.

This feeling inside of me reminds me of Grace of all people. The ache in my chest that creeps up out of nowhere. It's been two days since we had our moment and took that picture and all. Last night she came in for a moment, but didn't stay long. We were packed too. I barely had a chance to talk to her.

"You need a hobby, Charlie... a girlfriend." She adds the last part beneath her breath, but I heard it and the subtle dig in her tone. Giving her a side eye, I watch her as she grabs the aprons off the hooks and bundles them in her arms. Laundry.

Irritation settles deep in my chest. I don't need another woman telling me to settle down. God forbid I do get a girlfriend and she's just one more woman to point out all of my errors. I stare at the stacked boxes for a second and then realize I need the clipboard. It's been a long damn night, but it's best I get this taken care of before I place the next order.

I have to walk around Maggie to get to where I'm going at the side of the back room, farthest from the dining area.

"You know," Maggie calls out to me. I snatch up the board and pen from where I left them on my desk. "I really think you should hire a manager."

Her arms are still full of the aprons as I come out of my office. She blinks once and waits for a response.

It takes me a moment for her words to sink in. I don't have fucking time to find someone to help me, let alone actually train them and show them how all this works.

"I don't think so, Maggie," I answer her easily.

"I could find one. I could do the interviews and training," she offers as I look down the checklist, trying to focus. I read the same line three times as her offer hovers in the air.

No answer comes from me, not right now when I need to get this right. Three more items for the local beer truck and I rub my eyes and slap the clipboard down. It's a normal delivery, but a few brands just aren't selling. I'm not ordering them anymore. They're seasonal, and not many customers seem to be going for them.

Mags steps closer to me, crossing her arms and waiting for me to look up before she says, "You can't do this on your own."

"It's been working out so far." The words slip out, but my lighthearted playfulness is absent. Exhaustion weighing it all down. I know she's right and in the long run it would help. It's just that it's going to set me back right now to take someone on and spend time training him or her, moving slower than if I just did it all myself. Mags would probably hire a friend or family member. She's got a big heart and I love that about her. But hiring friends and family doesn't always work out. It causes even more problems. James comes to mind at that thought.

"You know you can't keep this up." Genuine concern laces her voice.

My mouth opens to respond with some kind of joke, something to put her at ease, but Maggie leaves before I get a word out. Practically storming out. I watch her back as she heads out to the front, the double doors swaying and creaking.

I've been doing this for years and it's worked out just fine. That's what I want her to get. But a piece of me knows she's right. All the long hours are getting to me. I suppose that happens as you get older.

The doors hold my attention as they slowly stop swinging. Rubbing the sleep from my eyes with my pointer and thumb and my hand across my face, I think again about how she's right. Just before I toss the pen down on the desk, I see the notification on my phone. Someone messaged me.

My brows pinch as I look at the number. I don't know it, and it's not programmed into my phone.

What should I wear to the wedding?

A smile curls my lips up. Grace. That's right. Now I remember.

Last night before my sweetheart left, I put my number in her phone. I wasn't sure if she'd use it or not, but I told her to.

I huff a small laugh at the text, remembering the night before. She was sweet after a couple more drinks, leaning on me a little more than usual. Asking if I was just messing with her.

If it was a few years ago, I may have thought of her as the clingy type.

Intending on grabbing my keys from my office to get the hell out of here, I lean against my desk and then decide to just fall into the chair as I look at her message again.

Two nights ago, I didn't have a single problem with her clinging onto me while the guys in the back shooting pool were looking at her. She didn't even notice them, and I sure as hell wasn't going to point them out to her. If I'm honest with myself, I would have rather spent last night with her the same as the night before, rather than working.

I'm too tired to think, but I text her back with the first thoughts on my mind.

It's a small wedding. Nothing too fancy or formal is fine.

It's been nearly an hour since she messaged me. I sit the phone down, thinking she won't get back to me for a while, but the phone goes off rapid fire.

Okay, so not a ballgown, got it.

I'll do something simple...

But classy.

What are you wearing?

The laugh comes up easy, vibrating in my chest. I lean back, and get comfortable in the chair. I'm so damn tired I could lay my head down right here on this hardwood or stack of paper and take a nap.

I text her back: *I'm in the wedding, so I have a suit. The groom is the only one in a tux.*

Her response makes me laugh even harder.

And you told me I could wear jeans!

With a wide smile on my lips, I respond: *Wear whatever you want, sweetheart.* I stare at my message for a second, playing with a small tear in my jeans before adding, *I'll be in gray with a dark blue tie.*

I can practically hear her voice when she answers: *Okay, now I've got something to work with.*

I grin at her message, debating on what to say back.

Probably nothing, I think as another yawn takes over. I'm too damn tired to keep going at this point. I stretch out and grab my keys, nearly pocketing my phone before it beeps again.

And you're sure you wanna take me?

I knew it. I knew she'd second guess it or think I was just fucking with her.

You backing out of our deal? I hope she can feel my smile when she reads it. I add: *We shook on this. That's as good as a legal notarized document when a handshake happens in my bar.*

I don't even notice Maggie come in until I hear her voice.

"Now, whatever's got you smiling like that," she says with her hands on her hips, "that's what you should be spending your time on."

I lift my head to look at her, but the second I do, my phone goes off.

I'll pick out something to match.

Chapter
NINE

Grace

"Oooh, let's go in here!" Diane says, tugging at my arm and pointing to a shop. "I'll bet they have exactly what we need." Ann is back and she decided the three amigos, as she refers to us, should go shopping. She didn't like the tension between Diane and me.

"Okay," I say easily, allowing her to pull me inside. I rub my inner elbow where I've just been poked and prodded. I had to have lab work done quickly before coming here. I'm hoping for the best, but prepared for the worst. At least shopping can take my mind off of this mess. Even if it's with Diane. Since Ann had to bail to pick up her son.

Seriously, Ann is killing me.

Diane came into work all chipper, like the fight we had Tuesday never happened. I'm sure that's Ann's doing and all, but if Diane doesn't like me, she doesn't have to hang out with me for Ann's sake.

Other than my small hesitation, I was happy to let it go and move on, because I had so much on my mind. Namely, *dress shopping* and filling Ann in on the details.

Now that she's gone, I'm just going to make the best of it. And honestly, Diane has been the version of herself that I actually do get along with. So… nothing but good vibes and positivity.

So after listening to Diane dish about all of her dating shenanigans, I admitted to her that I had agreed to go to a wedding with Charlie as a favor.

Diane actually squealed, which made me smile, then gushed about how she was going to the wedding as well. Apparently, some distant cousin of Charlie's or another relative was her new fling.

That conversation led us here, to what the sign proudly announces to be Dynamite Dolls. A quick look at the windows shows that the shop caters to '50s pinup designs, with two mannequins dressed to the nines in plaid pleated dresses that have a touch of class. I think it's the fit on them that does it. The pinched in waist and lines that hug the curves.

My simple, black work heels click on the shiny floor inside; the shop is obviously very nice – cue the word 'expensive', with fashionable dresses on racks on both sides as we walk in. In front of us is a wraparound counter, with two fully decked-out sales associates behind it. One of them is wearing a pair of earrings that I die for. Gold bumblebees dangle just beneath her ear.

An extremely petite blonde and a tall, plus-sized redhead behind the counter turn as we walk in, the one with the earrings, obviously stopping mid-conversation.

"Welcome!" the two say in unison with perfect smiles.

The blonde rushes out to the sales floor, beaming. It

seems that we're the only customers in the store, which is fine by me. I've never heard of this place but the vibe is very much my style.

I don't shop much at all in this part of the city. It's a bit out of my price range, usually. Given that this dress is for a wedding, obviously, I need to get something nice. Something to make Charlie swoon. It's a treat to myself, too. Because, why not?

"I'm Tessa. Are y'all looking for anything in particular?" the blonde asks. The rack of dresses made of black crepe catches my eye just as Tessa question us.

"Actually, we're both going to a wedding," Diane answers her and I stay mum, looking around. "So we need something classy..."

My fingers trail along the beautiful fabric; it's luxurious. As soon as I get to the price tag and turn it over, I can't help that my eyes widen, but at least the gasp is silent. Holy crap. Six hundred dollars for one dress? What the hell kind of place did Diane bring me to?

Blinking rapidly and trying not to show that I'm freaking out I know damn well I cannot afford this place, not in the least.

Of course, Diane has no idea that I'm stressed about money. Well, that is, I'm looking *forward* to being stressed about money.

Today at work, I Googled how much it costs to find a sperm donor and what the process is like. Then I nearly had a panic attack, because just the sperm can be hundreds of dollars. I remembered what my doctor said about IVF treatments... the cost of those can be *thousands* of dollars.

It took me a full three minutes of deep breathing to calm down from that one. I had no idea that going the donor route could be so expensive. I wasn't prepared for that, but I guess I'm going to have to face it. And the longer I wait, the more and more likely it will be that IVF is the only route left.

I frown as I drift to the rack across from me. I touch a bright red dress, almost scandalous with its low-cut neckline and daring side slit hem. I wish.

"Ooooh," Diane exclaims from just behind me. "It's perfect!"

"Oh… I don't know. It's not right for me, I think," I say absently.

Diane shoots me a look. "It's for me." She grabs the dress just beside the one in my hand, a different size, and passes it to Tessa, who beams at us.

"Oh," I say, shaking my head at myself. "Right." It sure as hell isn't for me at that price. Dress or baby? That's all I keep thinking. That and where is the sale rack.

I take in a deep breath and smooth out the sweater I'm wearing. The simple black cotton feels rough compared to the red number. Only positive vibes, I remind myself. Just happy thoughts… something in here needs to be on sale. Or… I bet this place offers credit cards.

"I'll get you a fitting room," I overhear Tessa tell Diane.

"Uh huh," Diane says, her attention elsewhere. "Oh, look at *this*."

Resisting my urge to laugh at Diane's giddiness, I move to another rack. Biting my bottom lip, I look up covertly and search for a clearance section, but there isn't one. Taking a deep breath, I try to loosen up a bit.

A flash of blue catches my eye, a hue just a bit lighter than the color of the ocean. I flip through the dresses until I find it. It's part of a slinky little silk number, classic and elegant.

My fingers grace the fabric of the dress and I smile at the

way it slips between my fingertips. I think this shade would be perfect. I'll match Charlie, but it won't look like I'm trying too hard to fit into the wedding party since it's all dark blues according to Charlie. *It's perfect,* I think.

"Do you want to try that on?" Tessa says, startling me.

"Yes please," I say, forcing a small smile as my heart settles. I haven't even looked at the price tag.

I really should take a peek before trying it on. Sometimes I fall in love a little too easily. But Tessa is already whisking it off to the fitting rooms. I follow behind her, to the back of the store. My brows raise when I see that the fitting rooms are the same size as the rest of the store, with good lighting and a gorgeous tufted ottoman in the center of the room and bar in the corner. Wow… this place is fancy. Someone put some real thought into the layout of the store.

"Right through here," Tessa says, gesturing to the stall and hangs my dress on the copper molded hook.

"Grace, are you in here?" Diane says, her voice reverberating off the stall walls.

"I'm right here," I answer back all sing song like, putting my purse down in my own stall and locking the door while staying positive.

"Oh, good. Okay, I'm trying stuff on. You'll tell me if it makes me look fat, right?"

"Of course," I call out, grateful we're the only two back here.

I know damn well Diane just wants her skinny ass complimented, she never looks fat in anything and I tell her as much. She only laughs in response.

I wriggle out of my sweater and shuck my skinny jeans. Unzipping the back of the dress, I glance at the tag but refuse to actually look at it before slipping the dress on over my boyshort panties and bra. I zip it up, reaching behind me and wiggling a little to get it all the way up.

My eyes travel the length of the mirror in the stall. Even barefoot, there is no doubt this dress looks amazing. I step closer, admiring the sweetheart construction. The dress is short sleeved and falls mid-thigh. It looks…

Damn. I'm afraid to really look at the price tag, because I *have* to get this dress. It's flattering in all the right ways. Charlie's never seen me in something like this. I can only imagine what he'd think.

I turn to the side, putting my hand on my stomach. My flat stomach. I imagine how it would look to be carrying a baby and watch my shoulders slump.

Shake it off, I warn myself. *Shake off the negative thoughts!*

It's funny, I always thought that I would be a mom, with three or four kids hanging off me at all times. In the past, whenever I pictured my future self, I always saw children with me.

I did everything I was supposed to do. I concentrated on school, and once I earned my degree, I got a good job. But somewhere along the way I missed the step where I just magically *find* a partner to share it all with, and who celebrates with me when I find out I'm pregnant.

Now, as I look at myself in the mirror, and for all my accomplishments, all I can see is what I lack. I can't look at myself and smile, because I know that there's a very good chance I'll end up childless. And if I eventually find Mr. Right, I can't give him kids. Oh my God these hormones have come out of nowhere.

I try to talk myself down from the crazy ledge I've put myself up on, but it's impossible. I turn just as Diane knocks at my door before trying to whip it open.

"What are you doing? Come look. I don't know about this one..." Diane says from behind the door. "I think I'm going to just pass."

Meanwhile, I'm trying to ignore the prick of tears at the back of my eyes, trying not to think of how cute baby shoes are, how I'll never have a reason to assemble the antique crib that my mother gave me.

I'm silently freaking out, and totally ashamed of it. It's only when Diane knocks on the fitting room door again that I'm able to pull myself together.

"Come look at this one," she begs me. "I think this is *the* one."

I wipe at my eyes and step out.

"That dress is gorgeous," she immediately replies staring at it as I walk out. Deep breath in. I do love this dress and it would be perfect. "Do you think they have it in my size?"

I frown. "For the wedding?"

"Yeah, I freaking love that dress."

"I think I'm going to get it," I answer her in a tone that signifies, hey, this one is mine.

"Oh. Are you sure?" she questions.

Taking another look in the mirror in front of us, this one far larger than the one in the fitting room, I nod. "Yes."

"Ugh. Okay. Well, what do you think of my outfit?"

She twirls in a circle. She's wearing a two-piece dress that shows off her mid drift made of a deep read twill.

"Beautiful," I answer honestly. "Not everyone can pull that off.

She blows out a breath. "Is it right for a wedding though?" she questions and I honestly wouldn't think so but I only shake my head mildly. I'm not sure I'd wear something with my midriff showing but I do think it's a laidback wedding and I really don't ever show my midriff.

"This shop doesn't have anything cute anyway." Diane's response shocks me as she walks off. She disappears back into her changing stall, and I do, too.

"Hey, are you ready? I think I want to stop at the food court before we go, get a sugar-free, fat-free froyo." Diane's voice is so full of happiness.

"Uh, just a second," I call out. I unzip the dress. "I'll be right there."

"Okay. I'll be looking at the jewelry."

I put the dress back on the hanger, listening to her footsteps fade as she leaves the fitting room area, then take a deep breath. I stare at the dress for a long moment, knowing that I won't find anything nearly as perfect anywhere else.

And I'll match Charlie. I'll look *good* next to him in this dress, like I belong with him. I'll look like I could be his real girlfriend instead of a pretend one.

I shimmy back into my jeans and sweater, then consider the dress once more. It only takes one more look at the dress before I scoop it up and head for the register.

They did offer credit card applications after all. So the dress is mine along with a new shiny store credit card I'll never use again.

Chapter
TEN

Charlie

My eyes drift to the entrance of the bar like they've done all night. I'm waiting for *her*. I'm eager for that shy smile to greet me and to watch her walk those sweet curves through the doors. I'm ready for Grace to act like she's not affected by me, as all the while that blush creeps up to her cheeks.

Checking the clock again and clearing my throat, the faint itch in my throat that's nagging me does nothing but irritate me.

I've been waiting all night. She's usually here by now. I'm not used to these nerves or waiting on anyone. Not like this.

The faint hum of the televisions behind me and the chatter in the bar keep me company as I go through paperwork, while sitting at a table. James is back on bartending duty. Occasionally, I peek over my shoulder, checking on him and propping my feet up on the chair across from me, trying to relax. Acting like this is any other night.

James has a charming smile as he talks with a few of the patrons. His uncle's here, Frank, in his normal spot. I'm sure James isn't going to act like a little shit with him here. This is his last chance after showing up late yesterday and forcing Mags to handle all those boxes herself. He's on thin fucking ice.

My chair scrapes the floor as I shift in my seat, trying to get comfortable in the back right corner. I've got a perfect view of the front entrance. I'm right next to the end of the bar. It's the closest I could be to Grace's usual seat.

Shaking my head, I wonder what the hell's come over me. Worked up over a woman. A woman I haven't even kissed. Haven't touched. A woman who isn't my girlfriend... Yet.

The papers rustle in my hands as I go through all the bills again. We're making a damn good profit and the return on investments are steadily on an increase when last year they were flatlined. I almost feel like I can breathe, like I can take a damn break, but I know it'll only take one hiccup to have something get fucked up.

Sitting up straighter in my seat and moving the soles of my shoes from the chair to the floor, I try to get this weird feeling to leave me. I need a beer. I need to relax.

I need my sweetheart to get her ass in here.

My gaze drifts to my phone, face down on the tabletop. My foot taps relentlessly on the floor. It's really not like her to be this late. It's almost eight o'clock.

As if staring at my phone will will her to call, I spend a long moment doing just that, debating on shooting her a text. She hasn't messaged me since the other morning.

I blow out a breath. It's not like any of this is real anyhow. It's just flirting.

Back to work, and letting go of all this tension, I lean back in my seat and grab my pen to tally up the bills in my record book. So far, so good. Everything's looking on point and within budget as I scribble down the amounts.

"Charlie, are these seats taken?"

My hand stops mid-stroke as I hear my mother's voice.

"He saved them for us," I hear Ali say. Tension creeps up my back. What the heck are they doing here?

My notebook lowers to the table with a dull thud as I give them both a tight smile. I don't know what it is about my family coming to my bar. Part of the reason I built this bar was to get them out of my mind. To get the whole damn town out of my head.

But I can never say no to Ma. Or to Ali. And the town fucking followed me here anyway. It's not like my bank account complains.

"Pull up a chair," I tell Ma. I lean over and let her kiss me on the cheek although my gaze darts to the entrance. Suddenly I'm grateful Grace isn't here.

I can feel her lipstick smudge on my cheek, and I wait for her to look back at the bar before I wipe it off.

"To what do I owe this pleasure?" I question them, not hiding the surprise and wariness. My eyes flicker to the entrance again, and this time it's a different kind of anxiety running through me. They saw her picture. If she walks through that door, I'm fucked.

"We just wanted to see you," my mother says in a sweet voice, but I don't buy her southern charm for a second. Setting her purse in front of her, both palms on the bright floral fabric, she adds. "Can't a mom just want to see her son?"

"You just saw me, Ma."

My mom smacks my hand playfully, "You know what I mean."

"Did you get your suit fitted?" my sister asks me, a real sense of urgency in her voice. Maybe this is just for the wedding. They aren't trying to worm their way into whatever Grace and I have going on. It's just the wedding, I convince myself and I would relax but… no, I did not get my suit fitted.

I nod my head once, but I can't look her in the eye as my mouth opens. Fucking hell. I scratch the back of my head, looking toward the door again and letting out a sigh.

"Charles Theodore," my mother scolds me, "you need to get your tux fitted!" She smacks me on the arm, yet again, but this time with the tall menu on the table. Her lips are pressed into a thin line, but luckily I don't have to respond.

"It's a suit," Ali says as she yanks the menu from Ma's hands. "I don't want tuxes." She says the last line as if she's said it a million times to our mother before and I know she has.

"I don't understand you, girl," Ma shakes her head, but there's a playfulness to her tone.

"Can I get y'all anything to drink?" I hear James over my shoulder, and I turn to take him in. He shouldn't have left the bar, but a quick look shows that it's just the regulars. And it's not like Maggie is going to come over here. Everyone knows Ma and Ali… and the rest of my family.

"No, no thank you," Ma says and pushes off the table, "we're having a late dinner down at Iron Grill." An immediate sense of relief comes over me as I realize they're leaving. "I just wanted to stop in and say hi to my baby boy."

I can't help the flaming blush rising to my cheeks. I'll be sixty years old and she'll still be calling me her baby boy, I know it. Ma and Ali stand first, Ali lamenting how she's starving with all this stress and that I need to get my suit fitted. Immediately.

Thank the good Lord they're leaving; standing up to give

them both a quick farewell hug I finally feel relieved. And that's when I see Grace walk in from the corner of my eye.

Fuck.

My heart hammers in my chest, and it beats even faster when Ali follows my line of sight and squeals.

"No way! Grace!" A wide smile accompanies Ali as she practically runs to greet a wide-eyed and surprised Grace a few feet from the entrance. Every red alarm bell goes off in my head. Ali's got her in a hug before Grace knows what hit her.

With Ma in tow, I scold Ali, "Let the woman breathe Ali?"

"So-" my sister lets a now-catching-on Grace go when I stop beside them, feeling caught in a trap. It was a coup. I know it and I stare at both of them, my mother and my sister, letting them know as much, but neither looks at me, all of their attention is on my poor sweetheart. *Shit.*

"Hi there, Grace," Ma's voice is lower than usual as she takes Grace in. Her eyes travel down the blush-colored blouse Grace is wearing, and a smile finally ticks up on Ma's face.

Damn right. There's not a single reason Ma shouldn't like Grace. She's smart and sweet from head to toe. And looking to really settle down.

Ma should like that, even if I don't.

"Hi," Grace looks between the two of them, visibly swallowing as she moves the clutch in her hands back and forth and then stares at me with a pleading look.

"Just go along with it, sweetheart," I whisper in her ear as I give her a small peck on the cheek, followed by a hug. All for show for my family. *Just go along with it. Please.* That little peck though. It does something to me. Something that lights up every nerve ending in me.

"Ali," I say, looking at my sister and then Ma, "Ma, this is Grace."

"It's lovely to meet you." Ma and Ali say almost at the same time before Grace can get a word out. The nervousness is coming off her in waves.

"Same to you," Grace says in a gentle tone as she smiles shyly and bites down on her lip. "You both look lovely."

"So like I started to say," Ali says quickly, "I know we have to go," she looks at Ma, giving her a look that says, *'we saw her, she's real, now let's go and not scare her off,'* and then back at Grace, "but I was wondering..." Her voice gets a little higher as she sways back and forth and looks like she's holding her breath for a minute.

Is Ali nervous? What the hell does she have up her sleeve?

"Would you like to be my bridesmaid?" Ali says quickly, and I swear all the blood drains from my face. My sister has lost her damn mind. Grace's pouty lips drop open slightly in surprise and before she can get an answer out, the words rush out of my sister's mouth, "It's a small, intimate wedding. Low commitment. Really not a huge deal in terms of setting things up or anything." Her hands wave animatedly in the air as she continues, "You don't have to even get a dress. The girls are all wearing their own thing. I just really would love it if you would be in it. You mean something to my brother and that means the world to me."

Grace's expression stays completely the same with the exception of her brows raising. I'd laugh if I wasn't mortified.

"It's less than two weeks away-" I try to cut in and give Grace an excuse.

"Nonsense," Ali says with a hurt look. "There's nothing to it." She shakes her head and gives Grace those puppy dog eyes that let her get away with murder growing up.

"I don't have time to really..." Grace swallows thickly and tries to say no, politely. I don't know why that makes a tinge

86

of hurt settle in my chest. Of course she should say no. That picture we sent them was a lie.

"It would mean the world to me," Ali repeats and reaches out and grabs Grace's hand, which Grace holds back. "I know this seems out of the blue, but it's just that Charlie hasn't had anyone serious in his life in so long and I really want to welcome you into the family. The numbers are uneven, too. Michael has an extra groomsman."

I close my eyes, completely embarrassed and mortified.

It's quiet for a moment, but as I slowly open my eyes I see Grace slowly nodding her head. "I am honored and would love to."

"Yay!" Ali squeals with excitement again, jumping up and down while hanging on Grace's shoulder. Shit, I feel like an asshole for dragging Grace into this. "I have a dress appointment next week if you want to come, you have to meet all my friends; they're dying to meet you. It's going to work out perfectly. This was meant to be. I just know it was."

Before I can tell my sister how ridiculous she is, she's dragging Ma out of the bar and as much as I want to tell them how crazy this is, I'd rather have them out of here as soon as possible. Grace stands in place, holding onto the clutch like it's going to save her life.

"Lovely to meet you both," Grace bids them farewell tucking a strand of loose hair from her bun behind her ear.

"It was nice to meet you too, Grace," Ma responds.

"I'll see you soon, Grace! Charlie give her my number," and with that last demand, called out over her shoulder, they're gone and I'm left alone with Grace.

Her mouth hangs open a moment in complete shock.

"You alright?" I ask her warily.

"I just... did I really just agree to be your sister's

bridesmaid?" Blinking rapidly, Grace looks between me and the now closed doors to the bar.

A smile forces its way onto my face as I see Grace look around her like she just got swindled.

"You did," I tell her easily.

"Holy shit," she says with a smile. "I need a drink... you're buying this time."

A chuckle leaves me, rough and low and I follow her over to the bar.

"You got it, sweetheart."

Given how my family can be, my sweetheart handled herself pretty well, but I don't know how we're getting out of this one...

Chapter
ELEVEN

Grace

It's late, definitely after five o'clock already. Darn it. Glancing into the cubicles in the office, I find them empty. I slide my headphones off and hit pause on the playlist that I listen to when I really need to focus.

I had a feeling it was getting late, but not this late. Flicking my gaze to the clock on my computer screen, I confirm it's almost six. Yep, it's past quitting time for most of my coworkers and now I'm here all alone. Physically separating myself from my work and letting out a long exhale, I push myself back from my desk.

I spent the day working up several new ads for a health food company who wanted the whole package. From billboards to Google ads and social media placements. I'm not going to lie; I think they're going to love them all. Their branding and messaging is solid. Still, it's always a good idea to sleep on it, and look at it with fresh eyes the next day. It's already six anyway; I can email the files for approval tomorrow.

When I stand up I have to crack my neck and back I'm so sore. And then I try to down the rest of my coffee but I find it empty. Oh how I wish Tracey were here now with a hot cup to keep me from falling over. I probably need some water to balance out the crapload of caffeine I put in my body today.

I head to the small kitchen to the right of the elevators, where they keep a filtered water cooler and stumble on Diane, who's talking with Elaine and Karan, two coworkers from a couple of floors up.

"Oh! Hey," I say, tossing my coffee cup in the trash can next to them. "I didn't realize anybody was still here."

"I saw you at your desk, but you had your headphones on," says Karan, a pretty girl of Middle Eastern descent. She has a bit of British in her accent, though it's slowly fading. "I thought it would be better not to disturb you."

"Yeah," I admit sheepishly. "Thank you; I appreciate it. I banged out three packages today and I'm wiped.

"Elaine was just telling us about getting hit on at the bar," Diane says. "Right, Elaine?"

Elaine is the new girl at our company. She has dark hair and porcelain skin, which turns bright red at Diane's statement.

"Well, I wouldn't say *hit on*," she stammers. "I was just saying, a guy I've liked for a while talked to me for a long time last night."

"Oooh," I let the word drag on, moving past them and grabbing a paper cup, "That sounds like a win of a night. How did it end? You get his number?"

Before Elaine can do anything other than shake her head,

Diane teases, "I hear that our Grace got asked out by that hot bartender Charlie."

I freeze with the empty cup in my hand. Everyone who knows Diane at all has been introduced to Mac's, and by association, Charlie. I shoot Diane a look as I fill the glass with water, but she ignores it. I like to keep some things private, but nothing is private with Diane.

"He asked you out?" Elaine says. "You have to tell us all about it!" She's far too excited, but it only makes me giddy. He did kiss me on the cheek. I nearly blurt it out, but feel a blush rise instead and take a drink of the cold water rather than speak.

"Yeah, 'cause Charlie is dreamy," Karan says, practically drooling.

I laugh trying to shake it off, "It's not that big of a deal." It really isn't. "I'm just doing him a favor really."

"Spill!" Diane says. "We all want to know how *you* managed to snare *him*."

My gaze narrows at the manner in which Diane just made that statement. How could a girl like me snare a man like him? Insecurity steeps through every inch of me slowly. I didn't. I couldn't. That's how. I'll be damned if that doesn't hurt to admit. I won't; I take another sip instead, pretending that the truth doesn't feel like stepping into a cold ice bath.

"Don't say it like that," Karan says to Diane before turning back to face me. "Jeez. She didn't mean it like that, Grace."

"Right," I chuckle and sip my water again, it's nearly gone already. With a careless shrug from Diane and a, "I'm just curious," response from her, the hurt turns to anger. I'm pissed at Diane, but there's no reason to start a fight over something so small. *Jealous much?* My inner voice snarks. I let the tension out of my shoulders as I grip the cup with both hands and lean against the counter.

"I'd still like to hear," Elaine says, blushing. "I mean, Charlie is grade A hot."

"So tell us," Diane commands.

"He invited me to his sister's wedding," I say. "It's not really a date—"

The girls howl appreciatively, which makes me smile. That bit of happiness coming back.

"He invited you to a wedding because he's trying to tell you how he feels!" Elaine says, excited. Elaine's blush is contagious, finding its way to my face. She's so sweet and is constantly reading those romance novels with hot men on the covers during her lunch break. She's a romantic at heart, but I like the way she thinks.

"No, he invited her because he knows that weddings are an amorous atmosphere, and he wants to get in her pants." Karan corrects with a growing smile.

"Ohh, psshh," I say. "He needed to get his family off his back, so he said he was bringing someone. And then he invited me. I'm telling you, it's decidedly not amorous and if he wanted to get into my pants he didn't have to go through all that."

"So you wouldn't mind if another guest put the moves on him, then?" Diane asks pointedly.

"I… It's not like…" I say. My body stiffens. What the hell has gotten into Diane? I swear some days I wonder why she even talks to me.

"Of course she would mind!" Karan protests for me. "Have you seen Charlie? Because he's got amazing biceps, and an ass that won't quit. Give the girl a chance to get some, Diane!"

"I'm just asking," Diane says, putting her hands up. "Speaking of that ass, I'm planning to go to Mac's tonight to see it in action. You in?"

"Definitely," Karan says.

"Sure!" Elaine adds.

"Umm…" I say, unsure. "You know, I'm just not feeling it tonight, guys." The idea of Diane anywhere around Charlie sends that spike of anger back. I don't need to see that, not with how tired I am and all these feelings that bubble up every time I hear his name.

"Are you sure? Your man will be there," Karan says with a twinkle in her eyes.

"She said she's not feeling it," Diane cuts in. "So let's let her get back to work."

"If you're sure…" Karan says.

"Totally," I say. "You guys have fun." I don't think I can handle being around Charlie right now. It's definitely an uneven relationship in terms of how much we like each other, and I can already see myself getting hurt. Neither of us mentioned his mother and sister after they left. It's like we're pretending none of it happened and we're just our flirty normal selves. *But there was that kiss.*

Chapter
TWELVE

Charlie

Eight o'clock passes.

Nine o'clock has come and gone.

My shift is done. I told them all I was heading out early, but here I am, still waiting. I was hoping to take Grace out to dinner. Somewhere other than here to make up for my sister and her antics.

But she hasn't showed. She didn't come in last night either, even though some of her coworkers did. I have a sick feeling in my gut telling me something's wrong.

I finally give in and reach into my pocket for my phone to text her.

"You alright?" Maggie asks me as the denim rubs against my fingers as I pull the phone out of my back pocket.

"Yeah, fine," I answer as she sets an order of wings down in front of Mickey. The sound of the plate hitting the table forces me to look up at her. She smiles as she scoots the plate closer to him and addresses me.

"You don't look fine. Go home."

I stare at her, but she doesn't back down. "I'm going, just making sure a friend's not on her way."

"A friend?" Maggie's eyes light up. "Your little Grace?"

I don't like how she says it with that teasing tone. As if she knows something I don't.

"Yeah, her name's Grace." I hold her gaze, but Maggie's not affected in the least.

"You go on and message her then," she says, then leaves a bit slower and a bit happier than she came. Out of habit, I take a look around and notice Mickey looking up at me with a smile. It occurs to me that word is probably getting around about the two of us. *Shit.*

I shift my weight and look down at the phone. This wasn't meant to be anything. She's just a sweet girl to flirt with. We don't want the same things. That last statement resonates and makes me feel like an asshole. *What the hell am I doing?* I almost put the phone back in my pocket. If Grace wanted to see me, she'd be here.

Almost. I *almost* don't message her. But fuck that, I want to see her.

I took the first night off that I've had in a long damn time to see her. Maybe I didn't text her, since I assumed she'd come in like she usually does, but I have the balls to ask her. Right fucking now.

My body heats as I type in the message.

Missing you, sweetheart. I'm getting off work and wondering where you are.

I regret sending it pretty much as soon as it goes on the screen. It's not like she's obligated to be here. I let out a heavy sigh, hating that all of this feels so suffocating. It's been five years since I… I don't even know what I'm doing. Asking her on a date, I guess. A real one, not just to be my fake date for a wedding.

Sorry Charlie, I went home tonight.

A frown tips my lips down, and that sick feeling comes back to me. I clear my throat and type back without thinking.

I was hoping I'd see you. Now I don't have a dinner date. :(
Again, I immediately regret my decision. A sad face? Really? Throwing my head back I grip my phone like I want to strangle it. What is it with this woman?

A dinner date? Or a fake dinner date?

I thought the food would be real… I'm playful in my text back, trying to keep the conversation lighthearted.

You make me smile. I can see her doing just that. Smiling as she reads the message.

Good, you should be smiling. You're too sweet not to be smiling.

It feels easy flirting with Grace. It always has. My chest feels light as I wait for her response.

I'm sorry. Not tonight.

Another date? I question. I don't think she'd be one to do that. She'd tell me. But I ask her without thinking. I need to quit it with that.

Nope. Just a lot of work to catch up on and I'm exhausted.

I think about asking her if she's seeing anyone, and making this thing between us official. But then I remember all the stories she's told me about her dates and looking for a man to settle down with. Clingy. I'm not ready for all that. I could at least ask her out to dinner though. Just to tell her thank you for putting up with my sister. Maybe sneak in another kiss.

Another night? I ask her.

She takes a minute to respond, and all the while I'm getting more and more anxious. Maybe I should take the hint, but I don't want to. I at least want to feed her.

Sure. I'd like that.

I'm smiling and thinking about going home when her next text catches me off guard.

What are we doing, Charlie?

What do you mean? I text her back almost instantly.

Fuck, even before she answers I know what's coming. Grabbing the closest chair and ignoring Mag's stare, I take a seat and stare at the phone, willing her to respond. I lean forward, my elbows on my knees and wait, rereading her question. *What are we doing?*

I knew my sister got to her. Why the hell did she have to come in here and mess up what I had going with Grace? Everything was easy, just going with the flow and taking it slow. Making sure I'm not going to hurt her.

We're just having fun.

I text her back before she can answer, my heart pounding in my chest. I lean back in my seat, the legs screeching as they slide across the floor and run my hand through my hair.

I feel like I'm in a little over my head. I stare at her response for a moment. That sick feeling was right. I knew it. She's not happy anymore just playing around. I don't blame her. She knows what she wants, and me fucking around with her is just causing problems for her.

What do you mean? I ask her, as my stomach sinks. I rub my eyes, feeling exhausted and hating myself. What did I really expect from her anyway? I huff out a breath and shake my head as my phone beeps and her reply comes through.

I'm not really sure what it means to just have fun with someone. It seems like I'm going to end up getting hurt and I'm not sure it's a smart thing for me to do. I'm sorry.

I feel like shit, looking fixedly at the phone in my hand. Brushing my hand over my head out of frustration, I look up and see James at the bar, staring at me as he fills a glass with ice. I nearly snap at him, feeling stressed out and pissed off, but he breaks my stare and looks away as soon as he sees me glaring back.

I suck it up and text Grace back. I knew this was a bad idea. We're looking for different things in life.

Are you still able to come to the wedding or do I have to tell my sister we broke up?

Shit that hurt to write. I ignore it all, knowing it's best though. Better to break it off before she gets hurt. Because that's all I'm going to do anyway.

She's quick to answer: *I'll still go with you. And just so you know, I really do like you.*

I know I should say something to put her at ease. I should tell her something to make her feel safe and comfortable. But I don't want to lie to her and worse, I don't want to lead her on. I'm not ready to get married and have kids or any of that shit. And that's what she's looking for. Especially knowing she may not be able to. I don't need a baby-crazy woman trying to lock me down… but it doesn't stop me from wanting her. At least for as long as I can have her.

Soon as this wedding is over, she'll probably stop coming here altogether.

Night, Charlie.

I swallow thickly as I look at the screen.

I type in a few responses, but delete them all. I'm not going to lead her on. I won't do that to her; she deserves better. I finally settle on something simple.

See you later, sweetheart.

Chapter THIRTEEN

Grace

The second I finally pull my headphones off at work, Diane calls my name. My gaze flicks to the clock before turning to see that she's ready to go for the day, her jacket already on and purse over her shoulder.

"Hey," she says, striding into my cubicle and leaning against the desk. "I don't want to ruin your productivity or anything, but it's almost seven. Our meeting went long."

She doesn't need to but gestures to the salespeople who I can see filtering out of the conference room. Rubbing under my eyes I slowly stand up, stretching. I don't know the last time I got up. I've buried myself in work all day. Another productive day.

"You're not interrupting," I answer her. "I just came to a stopping point, creatively. Perfect timing."

"Well, we're going to the Local. You should come, assuming you're not too busy with Charlie," she says, teasing.

At the end of the aisle I spot the gaggle of women gathering near Diane's cubicle and then glance at my desk. If I start on another project, I'll be here until midnight at least and I'm sure as heck not doing that.

"Okay," I say with both a shrug and a smile. "Why not?"

"Cool," her peppy tone is infectious. "We'll see you there. It's karaoke night!"

She shoots finger guns at me, and I can't help but smile. "See you there."

The traffic is heavy, and I end up with less time than I'd planned to refresh my makeup and take off my leggings, leaving me in a very short pale peach dress.

Rushing to get there before it's too late and everyone else is several drinks ahead of me, I let my hair down on the way to the Local. By the time I pull into the parking lot I look —well, at least respectable. The car door shuts with a loud click and I spot Diane instantly, who's waiting outside the bar.

Taking in the bar patio, I'm immediately unsure. There are six tables outside, every single one packed with twenty-some-things ready to party. They're loud, and a few are smoking cig-arettes. I rub my forearm as I walk toward Diane, feeling like this isn't exactly my vibe.

"There you are!" Her arm wraps around my shoulder, pulling me in close and I nearly stumble but have to laugh. "I need my drinking buddy. Claire's driving us home."

It ends abruptly as the loud noise of the bar hits me the second the door is opened and I nearly stumble again from be-ing pulled in by Diane. Inside it's madness, lots of little booths packed with people. I have to immediately flatten myself against the wall to avoid a waitress with a tray of drinks. Diane grabs me and pulls me toward the back, where some of our coworkers have managed to secure a table. *Thank God we have a table.*

"Look who's here!" she announces.

A rousing cheer goes up, but I assume it has more to do with alcohol than my arrival. I recognize all the girls at the table, but the only one I'm friends with is Ann, and she's at the other end. I need to move seats. As quickly as possible. Ann says something, shouting it even, but I have no idea what she said. I can barely hear the conversation continuing to my right.

I should tell Diane that I don't plan on being here long. I just want to blow off some steam before I head home. The conversation with Charlie last night still has me feeling like an idiot. I don't want to stay past the point of being able to drive myself home.

"Listen, Diane," I try to get her attention. I'm interrupted by the arrival of two pitchers of beer and a stack of plastic cups. Another cheer goes up from our table.

"Shhh," Diane says, taking it upon herself to pour me a plastic cup full of foamy beer. "Here, drink up."

"Actually—" I try again, but Diane is preoccupied. Turning to my one ally here is useless, Ann is wasted. It only makes me grin, happy that she has a chance to get out and have a girls night.

"Shots! How many of us are there? Seven?" Diane shouts absently, turning around and searching for the girl who just brought us the pitchers. "Where's the waitress?"

I settle back in my seat and sip my beer. *Don't be a party pooper*, I chide myself. I guess I'm just still down from the conversation last night. My phone buzzes.

I check it, and see that I have a text from Ann.

Good to see you, girl. I didn't think you'd come.

My gaze lifts to hers and I see her with her phone in her hand and the smile on her face as she stares back at me.

Good to see you too stranger! I have so much to catch you up on.

Tell me everything! But do it tomorrow so I'll actually remember.

A huff of a laugh leaves me at her response and instead of responding, I lift my cup to her in cheers and we drink together.

"Hey!" Diane says, snapping her fingers in front of my face. I wrinkle my nose at her, and she smiles. "Quit moping and drink already!"

Soon, not one, but two shots are put in front of me.

Everyone throws the shots back, one and then the other. I do the same, willing the alcohol to drown out all the over-thinking I'm doing. To my surprise, it actually tastes good, like a piece of grape-flavored candy.

"Mmm," I hum appreciatively. I sip my beer and try to fit in.

A night out and some alcohol definitely can't hurt even though I find myself thinking about Charlie. I don't know the first mistake I made. Making that bet. Or asking him what we were.

My phone buzzes again and I see it's from Ann. When I lift my gaze to hers, I see the concern. *More beer.* She wrote me.

I lift my glass again and pretend I'm not crazy. That I don't feel like I just had a break-up.

⟡

An hour later, we collectively heave ourselves out the front door and into Claire's car. I drank way too much. I knew it too, but each drink made the anxiety in my chest feel lighter and lighter. And I got to talk to Ann and tell her everything. At least I think I did. I'm not sure she heard it all though through all the noise.

There are six women packed in Claire's little Nissan Altima, but we're not going far. Mac's is right around the corner from here, and they've got a DJ spinning tonight.

There are three reasons really, why I'm going and that's what I think about in the car ride there. Although I make sure to laugh when the other girls laugh, clinging to my bottle of water Ann grabbed for me.

1. I'm too drunk to drive.
2. I didn't want to stay at the Local by myself
3. I want to prove it's fine; I'm fine. It was silly and nothing happened anyway. Everything is fine, so I'm going.

We get to Mac's in one piece, thanks to Claire being the designated driver. It's dark inside, with a couple of spotlights casting their glow on the bodies packing the dance floor. It's not nearly as packed as the Local, but there are more people in here than usual.

"Whoa," I say as I push through the crowd toward the bar. But then again, I come during the weekdays mostly.

Charlie's working the far end of the bar, serving drinks to what looks like a whole sorority's worth of girls. I follow Diane to the other end of the bar, where a younger guy is making drinks. Is that James, I wonder? I don't remember and my brain is hazy.

I try to think what his name is with every step, but it escapes me. I realize that I must be tipsy, so I try to rein myself in while I stand at the bar, although my eyes keep darting to Charlie, waiting for him to see me. There's not enough alcohol to make the bundle of nerves in my stomach knock it the heck off.

It takes a couple of minutes for me to get a drink. When I'm finally at the front of the line at the bar, I catch Charlie's eye. He looks at me first, then at my work friends, and sort of shakes his head. He's smiling, though. I bite down on my lip, feeling the smile stretch across my face as I rock on my heels.

But before I can even say hi, his attention is diverted back to the coeds, and he says something that makes them all titter. I'm certain one of them attempts to pull Charlie in for a kiss. He dodges the kiss at the last minute, but I've had my fill of watching.

It's just *fun*.

All that internal pep talk leaves me in a quick second.

I turn away, grabbing my drink, cheeks heating and my throat feeling tight. If Charlie can flirt with every woman who looks his way, there's nothing saying that I can't *have fun* with whoever I want. As if that's what I want to do right now. I dance my way over to Diane, trying not to let my hurt show. Well my attempt of a dance. It's more like I sway my way over to her.

It's not like you even have anything with Charlie, I remind myself.

I put my hands up in the air and dance, careful not to spill my drink. I'm sticking with beer tonight. Diane and the girls join in, and I try to just relax and have fun. I refuse to look over at Charlie, instead plastering my gaze on the back wall where the TVs display some music video.

It doesn't take long for the group of girls on the dance floor to draw more men in and for Ann to decide her time is up. She rushes out, her husband waiting for her in the parking lot.

With her gone, and Charlie... preoccupied, my mind goes exactly where I don't want it to.

It's crowded, it's loud and I feel like shit. In a room with all these people, I have to force the smile on my face and I just want to go home.

This was a mistake and the second I know that, I sneak out and get a cab home. Not looking back to say goodbye to the girls or to Charlie. I'll make up some excuse tomorrow but I just have to get out of there. I don't know what my first mistake was, but coming here tonight sure as hell was a mistake.

Chapter
FOURTEEN

Charlie

My alarm clock goes off, but I'm already up. I slap my hand down and the incessant beeping stops. I couldn't sleep for shit. The whole night, all I kept thinking was that I'm an asshole for trying to be with Grace without giving her a commitment. What's even worse is feeling like she's done with me.

She didn't say a word and she left the moment she got there. She's most certainly done with me.

I don't want to be done with her.

Sinking back into the bed, I stare at the thin opening between the dark curtains and watch the stream of light pouring into the bedroom. My only sliver of hope is that she said she'd go to the wedding. I don't know why I'm holding onto her as hard as I am. We haven't even kissed. She's not tied to me in the least.

The bed groans as I slowly slip off the edge and stretch my arms high above my head. I blow out a tired exhale as my bare feet pad across the wooden floors. They're cold, and I'm pretty sure the furnace went out last night. Every hair on my arms stands on end as goosebumps travel up my back to the base of my neck.

Damn, I hadn't even noticed. I grab my phone off the nightstand on my way out of the bedroom. I have to call her or text her. Something; I can't let her think I'm just some prick.

That's exactly how she looked at me last night. My heart thuds hard in my chest as I climb down the stairs, not bothering to grip onto the iron railing. I don't go around kissing random women. Maybe I did once, but that was a long time ago.

This house is old, built in the '30s and in need of a little more TLC. I bought it just before I bought the bar from Mac. I round the stairs in the foyer and take in the progress I've made. The slate flooring at the entry is fucking freezing against my bare feet. The furnace definitely went out.

I was able to get more work done on the house before I started spending all of my time at the bar. The first floor is completely remodeled, with new practically everything and fresh paint. Gray tones and dark blues are the theme throughout the open floor plan, including the black granite and steel backsplash in the kitchen. I spent all the money I had to make this place into the modern bachelor pad I wanted it to be.

But now when I look at it, it's just cold. Empty. Devoid of life. The lines are too straight, and the furniture practically looks brand new. 'Cause it's barely been touched.

The door to the basement opens up with a creak and I

switch on the light, a single bulb at the bottom of the rickety stairs. I never did get around to making the downstairs what I wanted it to be. A half-built bar is in the very back. Drywall's been put up and screwed into place, but I haven't spackled it yet.

I don't even want to finish it anymore; I think I just wanted to believe I was loving the bachelor life.

The truth hits me hard, like a bullet to the chest, but I keep moving, heading toward the furnace to mess with the electrical box. I know the right cords that need to be wiggled and tightened to get it to kick back on. I should get Joseph to come down here and fix this shit.

As I'm messing with the cords in the box, I think back to how pissed off I was when I bought this house.

It was the first one on my list. The realtor showed it to me, and I bought it right then and there. All the money that I had saved up for the wedding became a down payment instead.

The furnace clicks on with a loud swoosh and clink.

Shutting the thin metal door to the box, I stare at it as the fire burns high and the sound of air running through the house kicks in.

I didn't give a damn about anything other than getting as far away as I could without being so far that I'd lose my family.

Now here I am, all these years later, in a cold house, alone.

And pushing away the cute little sweetheart who made me happy for the first time in God knows how long. *Why?* Because I couldn't give her an answer to "what are we doing?" that she'd accept.

I kick the basement door shut, feeling more and more pissed at myself, and head to the island to have a seat and call her, but before my ass even sits, the phone goes off in my hand.

And it's her.

My breath stills for a moment, the only thought being that she's telling me she's not going to the wedding. I'll figure it out one way or the other, but she's coming. I'll make it up to her... but she's coming to that damn wedding, and I'm finally going to get a taste of my sweetheart.

I hit the button and answer the call.

"Hey there sweetheart," I say easily as if I'm not tense and waiting for her to try to back out of this. As if I'm not trying to figure out exactly what I need to say. I'm not letting her go. I've fucked up so much in the last few years, but letting her walk away from me before I've had a chance to make a move on her isn't going to be my next mistake. "Missed talking to you last night."

"Charlie," her soft voice pours through the phone, and the tone catches me off guard. It's apologetic. I hear her breathe into the phone. "Look, before you say anything, I just want to say, I'm very sorry. I shouldn't have told you off-"

Oh fuck no. I'm not taking this lying down.

"Sweetheart, you can stop right there." I can practically hear her sharp intake and see her sucking at her teeth. I've seen her do it before, when she's worried about something. The picture in my head of her doing it makes me smile and I relax against the island, the granite cool on my forearms. "You aren't backing out of our deal. You still haven't even told me what you want and I can tell you," I hesitate, remembering what she texted and feeling like this is a turning point and more importantly, like I'm risking hurting her. I'd rather risk that, than risk letting her go. Call me a prick, but I can't let her walk away again like she did last night. "I really like you too."

It's quiet on her end. Too quiet. I don't even know if she's still there. Doubling down, I tell her, "There I admitted it. Now you have me by the balls, Grace."

Her small laugh fills the phone. I can imagine her blushing.

"Well... I'll see you soon then?" she says, like it's a question.

"You better," I tell her.

"Alright then, bye Charlie." I realize as she says the words that I don't like her telling me bye.

"Bye, sweetheart." I don't like telling her bye either. The phone clicks dead and I drop the phone on the counter.

I shake my head. This is bad. It's real bad. I already like her too much. I already want to keep her.

Staring at my kitchen, I try to remember the last time I used it. I can't keep her because we have different life plans. The biggest problem though, is that I don't actually have a plan. Not one that makes me happy.

I text Grace on a whim, Do *you like funnel cakes?*

Chapter
FIFTEEN

Grace

I dress myself to go to the Piedmont Park Festival in a strappy linen-colored cotton sundress. It's my favorite. I twist around in front of the mirror in my bedroom, my mind on the upcoming event and a smile on my face.

It's an outdoor festival. I chew my lip as I try to decide on a jacket, since it'll be cool outside this early in the morning. A smile curves my lips up as I pick a light denim jacket, pairing it with light brown leather ankle boots.

I look in the mirror, and my expression twists. A pale redhead peers back at me, her blue eyes anxious.

Do I really look like that?

I need emotional support today, someone to lean on. I pick up my phone and scroll through the contacts and find Ann.

She's logical, whereas I'm… emotional. Although sometimes it's vice versa.

Without much time to waste, I put it on speaker once I get to my car.

"Okay, spill it." The first words out of her mouth make me laugh out loud.

"Spill what?" I rest my elbow on the car door and put my head in my hand as I drive down the interstate, listening to the GPS.

"You wouldn't call if it wasn't about Charlie."

"You remember what I told you?"

"How could I forget?"

Deep breath in. "Well, he decided I'm not allowed to back out of our deal and that he wanted to take me on a date," I practically squeal.

Ann's reaction is everything I needed. From the: oh my God, oh my God. To asking what I'm wearing and if I put on cute underwear... just in case.

The only time my smile slips is when I remember I haven't told Ann about the IVF and baby issues. In fact, Charlie's the only one I've told that to.

Ann wishes me all the good luck in the world, telling me she loves me and that she has such good feelings about this before I hang up.

When I park I have to remind myself, I'm on a date with my fake boyfriend.

A man who isn't right for me, and I know it. Heck, I doubt I'm right for him either.

A man who doesn't want the same things I want. That much we both know.

It's stupid of me. I'm wasting time.

But I can't help thinking he's a man who'd make a cute baby...

The chill in the air is more refreshing than cold when I get out to search for Charlie. Although I'm distracted, busy scrolling through an email on my phone. My doctor's office emailed me information about IVF and how to find a donor. My eyes widen as I look through it all. There are a ton of big numbers —ten thousand dollars, forty thousand unique donors.

It's too much for me to try to take in right now, especially if I'm supposed to be on this date. Stashing my phone, I wait at the entrance to the park, next to the big white sign waiting for Charlie.

When I see Charlie, everything in me clenches, the good kind of way. From his simple white tee pulled tight across his broad shoulders, to his bulging biceps and worn jeans… he is my kind of man. I try not to stare at him as I hand him an iced coffee, but his deep green eyes are all over me.

"Thanks," he says, eyes roving down my figure. "You look… *nice.*" Heat creeps up high in my cheeks, all the way to my temple.

"Yeah, well," I can't help but smile, blushing as I play off the compliment. I swear, when Charlie's around, my cheeks are a permanent shade of tomato red, made even more apparent because of my fair complexion. "You don't look so bad yourself."

"You ready?" he says, nodding toward the park.

"I am," I answer. I have to hold onto my coffee with both hands to keep from reaching out for his with one of mine.

Sipping my iced coffee, I ignore the feeling that something's different between us as we stroll down one of the paths, under a banner declaring this the Piedmont Park Festival in bright blue scroll. Each side of the path is dotted with individual booths full of food and games or larger showcases of handmade trinkets and art to buy, which take up several tents measuring twelve by twelve feet each.

I sip my iced coffee, but I can't help smiling as Charlie tells me a story about his younger sister Ali and how she had a fit one year over her funnel cake dropping.

"I mean… she was only, what did you say? Six? And I'd have a fit today if I dropped a full funnel cake."

The conversation is easy. The laughs are genuine. It's different. The small touches, the quick glances. It makes my naïve heart think there's something here.

"Alright, your turn. What about your family?"

"Well, it's just my mom now. My dad died in a car crash when I was little." I talk easily, but stare at the grass as we climb up a bit of a hill. I wish I had a big loving family like his.

"I'm sorry." I can feel his eyes on me, but I don't look back.

"It's been a long time. But thank you." It's quiet for too long. I want to tell him that I talk to my mom often but she's busy and travels a lot. It's all clogged at the back of my throat though, so I try washing it down with the rest of my coffee.

"What about your parents?" I question him, "What do they do. Your mom seems really sweet."

His grin is asymmetric and that's when our hands brush for just a moment. Ripping my gaze away so he doesn't see my blush get even hotter, I wait for him to answer. "Dad's a pilot. Ma's a homemaker. And you've met one of my sisters."

"That I have." I can feel my eyebrows raise up, remembering Ali. "I still have to message her," I admit to him. He only laughs and tells me he'll give me her number. I move the cold coffee cup to my other hand, wiping the water off on my jacket before taking another sip.

"What's Ali do?"

"She's a nurse. Just graduated two years ago."

I turn to look at him as we walk to the top of the hill and pause there, "And your other sister?"

"Cheryl's a homemaker, like my ma. She has a fancy English degree, and she'll probably go back to teaching at some point. She loves kids."

"Kids," I repeat the word, feeling a low tension roll over me.

"They have a baby now, so she's adjusting to being at home and all that."

The mention of a baby makes my heart flip. My lips part to ask him more about his sister, but my eyes catch sight of exactly what I want right now.

On cue, my stomach grumbles with hunger, "Want one?" I question

"The pickle on a stick or the waffle fries?" he questions, grinning from ear to ear.

Shrugging I answer, "Either or both." Fried food and big pickles on a stick are exactly what I think of when I think festival. That and funnel cake of course.

"Well what are you getting?" He asks me and I answer, "The doughnuts. They are fried heaven with powdered sugar." My stomach grumbles again as the smell gets stronger and the line we're standing in gets shorter.

Charlie takes his time, eyeing the menu written out on the board to the right of the stand. "It's kind of like funnel cake, but in ball form." I whisper getting closer to him, as if it's some big secret I'm confessing.

"I guess I'll take one and I want the whipped cream too."

I order easy enough and reach into my clutch, ready to pay since I offered. Charlie beats me to it though.

"Hey," I protest watching him hand over the cash. "It was my treat," my tone is wounded.

"Nonsense," he answers, taking the change and then both of our paper boats of dusted donuts. "It's my date," he nods and passes me the fried deliciousness I've been craving.

"Well thank you."

It's obvious by the way his lips part that he was going to say something, but a bit of cream slipped off the top of a hot donut and hits his wrist.

I must be crazy, because Charlie licking off that dollop of whipped cream turns up the temperature around me to about a thousand. A second passes as we step out of line.

My body heats, igniting with desire as I bite my lip, and see his gaze drop to my lips. I suddenly realize that I want him to kiss me. No, *need* him to kiss me.

I lean in just a fraction, rising on my tiptoes to kiss him and close my eyes, his lips mold against mine. The touch is electric, filling my whole body with a restless energy. The kiss is slow, not pushing for anything more, but that just makes it all the sweeter.

When we pull away, my whole body is covered with goosebumps, my breathing labored.

What really gets my heart racing, though, is the fact that the same expression is on his face. Our eyes meet, and it's so intense that I wimp out.

I look away and laugh, and the tension breaks.

"Is that how you say thank you for donuts all the time?" he asks mildly. "I could add these to the menu."

Another laugh leaves me at his joke. "Maybe," I say with a shrug.

Silence stretches, but it's easy. Everything suddenly feels easy and like it's supposed to be this way.

I try not to think of the details because, right now, it's just perfect.

Chapter
SIXTEEN

Charlie

As I walk Grace back to our cars, I can't help thinking that I don't remember the last time I took a day off. There's a reason I work my ass off.

I go after what I want, and what I want right now, more than wanting the bar to be stable, is *her*.

I lean close to her ear, letting my warm breath tickle her neck and sending goosebumps over every inch of her body as I ask, "You have a good time tonight?" The sun's setting, the crickets are out, and everything about this moment is picture perfect.

"You know I did." Her shoulders shake with a soft laugh and she pushes me away slightly, a bit of space coming between us as we walk through the grass of the park. I'm quick to close the gap, grabbing her hand and giving it a squeeze before pulling her back to me.

"Does this count as a first date?" my voice carries through the dark night.

"A date? All you asked was if I wanted funnel cake," she answers with a wide grin as she looks straight ahead.

"Well who doesn't love funnel cake?" I respond without thinking.

Grace rips her hand from mine, covering her face with a laugh before shaking her head. I love that sound. She practically skips a few steps to get back to me, that beautiful smile still etched on her face. My chest feels warm and full.

But I know this is temporary unless I do and say the right things. Committing to things in life that I am not ready for. It feels like a date, but a girl like her needs more than a hot dog, cola and fried donuts.

The night's still young.

The clouds seem to dim a bit more as the noises from the people leaving the festival behind us fade. We're some of the last people to leave.

Grace clears her throat in a polite fashion as we pass the last tent. The sky's darkening and dry lightning is in the far-off distance, brightening the horizon before leaving us in darkness with a loud crash. It's comforting though, and each time it happens, Grace steps a little closer to me. Her small body practically molded to mine as we leave the festival and head to the parking lot.

I love the warmth of her body, the feminine sounds of her gasps every time the lightning cracks across the sky. It doesn't take any effort at all to wrap my arm around her waist and pull her closer.

It's a real date, whether she wants to admit it or not.

I don't miss the way she perks up and deliberately avoids looking at me the second my skin touches hers.

"Did you have fun?" she asks me shyly. I like this side of Grace. At the bar she lets herself go sometimes, but mostly she's just joking to hide the real her.

She has a shit day, it's just a joke.

She's in a fight, she laughs it off.

But that insecurity is always there just beneath the surface. Out here in the open without the dim lights of the bar and alcohol, I'm not letting her get away with hiding anything. I want to know the real her. And I'm not holding back in the least.

It's different, and I like it. I want more of it. I want more of her.

"I did," I smile down at her as we walk through the path and finally reach the skinny sidewalk that leads us towards the cars.

The parking lot is at the very front and there's relative privacy from a row of trees that lines the sidewalk. It's late and dark. The sound of a car starting up leads my eyes to look straight ahead and watch the passengers drive off. Other than that, we're leaving the world behind us as we head home.

My jaw ticks and I tighten my grip around her waist as I realize we drove separately. Dammit. My fingers tighten a bit on her. I don't want this to end. I don't want to leave here and never get this side of her back.

I just need another date. The wedding.

The anxiety squeezing my heart fades as I realize I still have her. I still have a chance to give her what she needs to stay with me.

I can hold her for a little longer, get to see more of this side of her. She's looking for Mr. Right, but I can keep her occupied until he comes along.

Crack!

"Oh!" Grace jumps slightly as we walk across the pavement and she nearly falls. A rough chuckle tickles the back of my throat as I hold her closer. She's even more tempting in my arms.

She doesn't leave my hold right away, her soft blue eyes looking into mine. Her breath comes in faster, and it makes her breasts rise with each short intake. I can feel the spark between us, the pull that's ignited and pushing me closer to her, wanting to feel more of her, *all of her*. It's not until the steps of other attendants leaving the festival get louder, as the people get closer, that she pulls away.

She tucks her hair behind her ear, breaking my heated gaze and brushing it off like what just happened wasn't affecting her.

I can hear the smartass comment, the joke coming out of her mouth before she even says it. But I turn her in my grasp, gripping her hips and pulling her to my hard chest and crash my lips against hers. Silencing whatever was going to come out between those sweet lips.

I want her and she's going to know damn well that I do.

At first her lips are hard, caught by surprise, but she molds them to mine and parts that sweet seam, opening her hot mouth for me. She moans as I deepen the kiss, her small hands gripping my shirt.

I don't want to leave with only that little blip of a taste of her. The way her car's parked near mine gives us a bit of privacy. I want her to know what I can give her.

She may want marriage and babies, and I'm sure as fuck not ready for that... But I can get her addicted to something else.

More than an innocent kiss.

My hands grip her hips and I hear her ass smack against

my car as I splay my hand across her back and pull her against me. My dick's hard in an instant.

I don't know what happened. One minute she's all for it, kissing me back with just as much passion.

The next, she breaks the kiss too soon, the moment gone as she steps out of my grasp and leaving me pining after her. There's a chill between us.

"We're just friends, right?" Grace's voice is soft, full of feigned strength, the vulnerability shining through. "This is just fun?" Her eyes dart up to mine as she starts walking to her car, her heels clicking on the pavement as she tries to catch her breath and blow off what just happened. I quicken my pace to catch up to her and hold her in my arms, searching her face for the reason she just took off.

It takes me a moment to even register what she asked.

I know what she wants to hear. She wants me to say I want more. But the words won't come out.

The last time I gave someone more, she ripped my heart out. All I can see in front of me is how much of a fool I was back then.

Grace wants more, but I can't give it to her.

I pull away from her, forcing a smile on my lips and ignoring her question as I say, "I had a really good time tonight." *Fucking hell, what's wrong with me?*

Her eyes flash with something, and the shame of knowing she wants more but deliberately not giving it to her presses against my chest. She turns to leave without another word.

The dry lightning turns to rain as I watch Grace walk away. The droplets are light at first, warm. I don't do a damn thing to stop them from coming down as I unlock my car. It soaks into the thin cotton of my shirt, making it stick to my skin as I climb in and close the door.

She wants to be more than friends.

She wants a commitment, but she's already talking about kids.

I'm fucking crazy for wanting her. But I can't help it. I'm not stopping until I'm deep inside of her making her scream my name. She'll let it go then. It won't matter if there's a title on us or not. I'll make her happy. I can do that.

Chapter
SEVENTEEN

Grace

S itting in traffic, rubbing my temples, I let out an agitated sigh. Traffic is nearly at a standstill. I could get out of my car, go get a cup of coffee, and come back to find that traffic hasn't moved at all.

It's been a long day. A long week, actually. I laugh a little to myself because it's only Wednesday.

My goodness. I really need to unwind.

This past weekend… Charlie. My grip on the steering wheel tightens as I let out a strangled breath. What was I thinking? I'm playing with fire. He wants a good time and that's all I'll be to him. How much clearer could he make it for me? It's as clear as day.

But a good time is starting to look real attractive to me.

The image of Mac's Tavern comes to my mind, unbidden. Charlie, behind the bar. He's wiping down the counter. He looks up at me, and smiles when he recognizes me. And then he starts taking off his shirt...

A smile stretches slowly across my face and I actually giggle ridiculously. The fantasy is sweet and innocent. A lot sweeter than my day has been, at any rate. The fantasy is also unrealistic... just like my other thoughts regarding our relationship.

I chew on my lip. I wasn't planning on going to Mac's today, but... seeing Charlie would be nice. I feel good when I'm with him. There's no label or commitment though, and that makes me feel like a damn fool. After our date though, I couldn't care less about how it looks. I just want to be happy.

While I'm stuck in traffic, I manage to change out of my office attire, a gray pencil skirt and a white silk blouse. I pull a pale blue dress, strappy and knee-length, out of the back seat.

I try not to make eye contact with the people in nearby cars as I sneakily slip out of one outfit and into another. They're getting a free show, but nothing more from me. It's not like my bra shows any more than a bikini top anyway. My knee smacks against the steering wheel and I let out a sharp hiss. Ouch!

I have to shimmy the dress down over my ass and nearly hit the gas pedal, but I got it done.

I smile at myself in the rearview mirror and reach into my purse so I can put on some lipstick. A deep red, not my usual color, but it looks nice with the dress and brings out the blue in my eyes.

Not that I'm dressing up, or anything... I tell myself and then grin like the Cheshire Cat. Is it so wrong to do this with Charlie? My ovaries might say 'yes, yes it is,' when I'm at the doctor's but they don't have any objections when Charlie's kissing me. I know that much.

The parking lot is nearly empty by the time I finally get to Mac's. So empty that I think it may be closed, but it doesn't stop me from taking a peek inside. When I open the doors, it's vacant inside as well, the soft hum of the TV is the only sound. I turn around and check to see if there was a sign on the door. Maybe I missed that they're not open somehow.

But no. There's no sign. Just a big empty bar.

I walk across the floor, aiming for the back hallway that Charlie is always disappearing into. I chew the inside of my cheek nervously, knowing that I probably shouldn't go back there. My heart's beating faster at the prospect of being alone with him in his bar. It's definitely marked "Employees Only" for a reason.

But the bar is empty. There's no one to see me do it, so it doesn't really count. I remember how he kissed me the other night, and that's all I need to get my feet moving.

Navigating past the walk-in cooler and stockroom, I poke my head inside each to make sure they're empty. I continue back down the hall, getting more and more nervous.

Finally, I spot him. Coming to an abrupt halt, I watch Charlie in a small office, leaning over a desk full of paperwork. For a second, I'm too shy to announce my presence, so I just stare. He's nothing but trouble. But I knew that. Right from the beginning, I already knew it.

Charlie's wearing dark jeans that probably mold perfectly to his ass, and a dark t-shirt that fits snugly over his hard pecs and abs. He's hard at work, a pen in his mouth. I lick my lips nervously, strangely jealous of the pen.

The nerves start building when he doesn't notice me, and I can't take it. I clear my throat. "Ahem."

Charlie looks up, surprised. "Hey," he says, dropping the pen. It lands in his hand but he's quick to drop it.

A gentle smile, joined with a warmth that flows through me, creeps up on my face. "Hey. The bar is empty." I lean against the doorframe, not looking away from him. "I wasn't sure if I should come back here or not."

I don't miss how his eyes travel down my body before he answers. "Yeah. There's some free festival that's going on downtown." He shrugs. "Everyone left a bit ago. I didn't want to lock up though... just in case."

"Ah. Well, at least you've got one customer," I say, feeling more and more naive. He's busy. He's working. And I came unannounced. *But he didn't tell me to leave.*

My breath hitches when Charlie stands up, tall and with his masculinity on full display. I try not to stare at him, at the way he moves toward me.

"Well, if I've only got one, at least you're a pretty customer," he teases, flashing a grin.

I can't help but be dazzled by him. He's so handsome, with his deep green eyes. This is how he got me. I know it is. I'm struck by the air around him, the ease of everything about him and the charming way he looks at me, but the rough cadence when he speaks. He's the perfect mix of what I want if I could pick everything out on a checklist. I could get lost in those twin pools, swim deep below the surface of them. I already am lost. I know this is bad, but I can't help myself.

I open my mouth, but nothing intelligible comes out. "I... uh..."

Charlie comes nearer. This close to me, I can see the desire in his eyes. It almost melts me where I stand.

"I was thinking..." he says, brushing a coppery lock of my hair back behind my ear. "About the other night, at the festival."

His chest is almost touching mine now. I can feel a tingle of anticipation begin there, hardening my peaks.

"Oh?" I whisper breathily.

His big hand caresses my shoulders, warm fingers kneading my muscles. My eyelids flutter closed as he touches me. It's all I can do not to moan.

"Mmmhm. I think you need to unwind," he says. "You're so tense all the time."

"And you have an idea of how I should unwind?" I say, opening my eyes. I already know what his idea is. I had the strength to walk away at the park... but like a moth to a flame, I came right back.

A wicked grin lights up his features. It makes my toes want to curl.

"I do. I think you just need to get laid."

I suck in a breath, looking up at him. His eyes are searching mine, looking for an answer.

"Maybe I do," I barely breathe knowing I'm the one caving between the two of us.

The second the affirmation is out of my mouth; his lips are on mine. He spears my hair with one hand, and puts his other hand on my lower back pulling me to his chest, and taking what he wants from the kiss.

I press myself to him, molding us shoulder to hip, feeling the faint beginning of pleasure running through my heated blood. I've wanted him for days. He gives me a little of what I want with firm sweeps of his tongue against mine.

It's not enough, though. It can never be enough with Charlie.

"More," I demand, my voice rough. I know what I'm doing and there isn't a piece of me that doesn't know what this is. I want him. Plain and simple. Regardless of what happens tomorrow.

In a swift motion, Charlie picks me up, closing and locking

his office door in a heatbeat, his hands wrapping around my thighs and making me squeal in surprise. He knocks over a cup of pencils in his haste to settle me on the desk. I hear papers drifting to the floor, but I'm too wrapped up in him to look.

I'm breathless, nervous, but more than anything... I'm wanting. Skin on skin, more of his lips on mine, more of him, taking me.

He fits himself between my legs, pulling down the straps of my dress. I'm busy trying to get his t-shirt off. He finally growls and steps back, ripping the t-shirt over his head.

Running my hands all over his warm muscles, over his shoulders and down his back, I knew he'd feel like this. He pulls the top half of my dress down and nearly rips my white lace bra off; he's so eager. I guess we're both wanting.

In only a minute, I'm naked from the waist up, completely bared to him. My breathing comes in ragged. This is so wrong, but I don't care anymore.

"Fuck," he says, cupping my breasts with his hands. "You're so damn beautiful, Grace." There's a sense of awe in his voice that I wish I could focus on, but his deft fingers have my head thrown back in an instant.

When he tweaks my nipples, sharp shocks of pleasure and pain shoot straight to my clit and I gasp, thrusting myself deeper into his hands as my back arches.

"Yes," I moan. How long has it been? Too long. Far too long.

I only look back at him when he bends down to take my nipple in his mouth. I grip his head and groan, unable to process the sensation of his tongue on my flesh any other way.

Rucking up my skirt, he reveals the white lace thong I'm wearing. He kneels and kisses my knee as he pulls down my panties, casting them aside.

I try to close my knees, but he *tsks* at me.

"Open your legs for me," he commands, glancing up at me.

The hunger in his eyes is undeniable. I slowly part my thighs, holding his gaze. There's something so erotic about it, something taboo. It sends goosebumps down every inch of my body.

Charlie pulls my ass to the edge of the desk, and I tense a bit. Nerves pricking along my skin. Using a hand on my stomach, Charlie gently reclines me, whispering to 'relax'. He trails kisses up the inside of my thighs raising heat everywhere on my body. Scorching me and forcing my hips to undulate. His splayed hand warns me to stay still.

He teases me before his kisses reach my pussy, trailing down the seam. I shift in place as he uses two fingers to part my lips. I've never been like this with a man. So close and intimate. With my eyes open, I stare at the ceiling, barely seeing a thing and feeling every single thing. When he stops, I glance down at him, my lips parted and my chest rising with heavy breaths.

He looks up at me, like a tiger looking at his prey. There's a self-satisfied look on his face.

"You're so wet for me," he says. "That's so fucking sexy."

I blush and nearly cover my face but my hands close into fists instead. In the next heartbeat, Charlie kisses me right on my clit. It's electrifying, the feel of his lips like hot lightning running through my whole body.

He flicks his tongue over my clit a few more times, each flick making my body spark with need, then he swirls his tongue over it. Finally, he seals his mouth over my clit and I cry out, my hands flying to his shoulders.

"Charlie! Fuck!"

He moans, the vibrations forcing my toes to curl, and he does it again and again. I close my eyes. I grip his shoulders, his hair. It feels so goddamn good, I never want him to stop.

But before the heavy wave of my release crashes, he stops.

My gaze whips down to him, needing more and not knowing why he stopped. Charlie eases back from me, wiping his mouth. I open my eyes and look at him, wild-eyed. He chuckles as he stands up again.

"Relax, sweetheart," he says. "I'm not done with you yet."

I pull him to me, kissing him hungrily. As I take my kisses, he unbuttons his jeans, pushing them down part of the way. I gasp and pull back; he's freed his cock, and it's massive. Long and thick, and resting against me.

I look him in the eye, awestruck. He smirks.

"You thought I couldn't back up my teasing?" he says.

I bite my lip and reach for his cock. I can't close my fingers around his girth, that's how big his dick is. I know two things right this second.

1. I'm going to feel this tomorrow.
2. I have to tell Ann. Don't kiss and tell isn't a rule when you're with someone who's... well got something worth telling.

I caress him, feeling the warmth and steel of his cock beneath my fingers.

Mostly, I'm wondering how the hell he's going to fit. I hear crinkling, then realize he's unwrapping a condom. He kisses me, distracting me while he puts it on.

I lick my lips and almost remind him. The odds of me getting pregnant are slim to none. My throat starts to close with the emotions creeping up on me. All this bullshit that's been making me so crazy is getting in the way of my happiness yet again.

I won't let it. I don't have to tell him, and I'm not ruining this.

He takes his cock in his fist, and the sight of him touching himself gets me hotter than ever. As he positions himself snug between my thighs, my heart beats faster. I part my legs wider as his cock pushes against my entrance. He stretches me slowly and my head moves from one side to the other with the stinging pain.

I shiver, a chill running up and down my spine. Charlie brings his free hand up to cup my breast, the rough pad of his thumb brushing against my hardened peak, as he begins to push inside. I moan as he fills me, stretches me, possesses every single inch of my pussy.

"Charlie," his name is a strangled whisper from me. My eyes close, and my head falls back at the sweet sting of him pushing himself steadily into me.

"Say my name again, sweetheart," I hear Charlie say in a lowered voice.

Before I can do as he told me, he slowly withdraws, leaving a deep need in the pit of my stomach then thrusts into me, hard. My unintelligible groan speaks for me as he does it again. I grip the edge of the desk as a cold sweat breaks out over my skin and my body begs him to move.

"Goddamn," he groans with pleasure. "You're so fucking tight, Grace."

Fuck, it's so good. His gaze on me should be uncomfortable, but it's not. It's the hottest thing I've ever felt. His pace is steady, his thrusts deep. Each hard pump of his hips makes my body jolt, and I struggle not to fall over the edge. Over and over, my body feels hotter and hotter as I climb higher and higher.

Still, I sense that he's holding back, waiting for me to

finish. I don't want him to hold himself in check. I don't want him to busy himself thinking of me. I want him unhinged, out of his mind with lust.

I hook my legs around him and dig my heels into his ass, moaning into the crook of his neck as he hits the back of my walls, a sinful mix of pain and pleasure. With a rough groan of desire, he grips my hips and hammers into me, my screams of pleasure getting caught in the back of my throat. I can barely breathe, the intense wave of arousal climbing higher and higher. I don't even realize I'm not breathing until I let go of the exhale. It feels like something white hot is blooming inside me, something terrifying, but I fucking want it.

"Yes," I urge him on. "Do it like that, Charlie."

He kisses me hard, demanding more from me.

He lets loose, fucking me with crazed abandon. More papers fly off the desk, forgotten, but they're in my periphery as my head thrashes. My body is on fire and then too cold and needing more of his touch.

I rock my hips against his brutal thrusts, yearning for more.

I can feel myself tighten around Charlie, and I think he can feel it, too. He pulls my knee up, increasing the pressure, making me hotter. *Oh. My. God.* I'm right on the edge, desperate to go over...

Just as I think I can't, it's too much, Charlie makes a low sound, rumbling through his chest. Suddenly I'm in freefall. I swear I see stars, thousands of stars of every color. I cling to him as I find my release, burying my head against his neck. He rides me through my orgasm, ripping through me and only making the crash that much sweeter. My nails dig into his skin as his hot breath travels down my body.

He thrusts one final time, uttering a curse as he comes.

I hold him, and cling to him as his legs shake for a second. He stills, then runs a hand down my back. We're both out of breath.

My heart pounds as I raise my head to look at him.

There really aren't words that describe how amazing that was, so I try to put it in a kiss. It's short; he breaks it to breathe, but his large hand cups the back of my head, and then *he kisses me*. Deep and sweet. It's everything I want and need.

After another moment, he withdraws gently.

I wonder if sex is always like that for him. Wild, rough and demanding. Both people finding their pleasure together.

I've never had that before, not ever.

He kisses me again, cupping my cheek. Then he disposes of the condom and pulls his pants up. I pull up my dress, wiggling off the desk and slipping back into my thong.

I just want to be happy. I want to have it all.

Charlie smiles at me as he buttons up his jeans.

I've never settled for anything in my life. But I could settle with Charlie.

Even if it's not the same for him. Even if it's just a good time. I try to convince myself of that, but if it were true, then I wouldn't feel this sick feeling now that it's over.

Chapter
EIGHTEEN

Charlie

"I need the needle-nose," Joseph's voice snaps me back to the moment.

I clear my throat, feeling like a fucking pervert for getting lost in the memory of Grace's sweet curves while I'm only a foot away from my brother-in-law.

The rusty toolbox sitting on top of the wooden workbench opens with a bit of protest, and I grab the pliers for him.

"Yeah, here you go." Stepping back, I let him finish up the job on the furnace. I got lucky that Cheryl married a mechanic. "Thanks for coming and doing this for me," I thank him for at least the second time today as I grab the six-pack we brought down then take a seat at the bench. I crack a can open, and the snap and fizz fill the silence. "I know you don't have much time-"

"Shit," he cuts me off, and his response has my ass right

up out of the seat thinking he sliced his hand open or something. The look on his face tells me he's fine; he tosses the pliers on the bench and wipes his hands on his jeans. "I'm happy to get out of the house for a minute."

He gives the box a look over before shutting the metal screen and flipping the switch back on. The furnace roars to life as he sags down into the seat next to me. "You ever hear of colic?" he asks as he reaches over and grabs the beer I offer him.

"Colic?" I have no fucking clue what he's talking about.

"It means your baby cries… a lot."

A grimace appears on my face and if I'd have to bet, it matches his. I focus on my beer and he focuses on his.

Joseph and I hit it off when he and Cheryl started dating. I never did like her previous boyfriends, but he treats her right. He's a good fit for her. A good husband, and a good father. Even though he's working his ass off while Cheryl's out on maternity.

"Sorry to hear that," I tell him, the beer right there at my lips. I don't know what else to say. I don't know shit about babies.

He lets out a heavy sigh, "It's alright." His eyes are distant when I look at him. He's got a few days' worth of scruff and I'm only now noticing the dark bags under his eyes. He huffs out a small laugh and takes another sip of his beer.

A chuckle leaves me at his next comment, "My ma said it was karma for how I was as a baby."

With a long sigh, he adds, "She's a daddy's girl, though." A sparkle hits his eyes, and I finally ease up some.

"Yeah, that's what Cheryl says."

Wiping his forehead with the back of his hand he takes a seat beside me. "At like two in the morning, every morning, she's up and hungry. She doesn't want me then." He makes a face with wide eyes and it makes me laugh as he takes another drink. "But any other time, she's my baby girl."

The pride in his voice makes me smile. "I'm real happy for you two."

With a nod and a smile still on his face, he admits, "I always thought you'd have one first."

I grunt a response, "I'd need a woman to make that happen."

"You had one when I first met you." My body tenses some. I know Ma's always bringing it up around everyone. She's always pushing me to settle down, but I don't need to hear it from my brother-in-law. I only put up with it from Ma, cause she's my ma.

"I'm just sayin'," Joseph takes a deep drink. "You'd make a good dad, if you ever wanted to."

That's my cue to stand up and stretch; I do without looking Joseph in the eyes. "Yeah, well. Maybe one day."

I take a few steps to head upstairs, but turn when I don't hear Joseph following me. The site of him is nothing but casual although he's looking at me like he's waiting for something.

"I heard you got a woman."

I run my hand over my face with frustration. Why does everyone have to complicate everything and get into my business? I don't need anyone in my head or trying to push things one way or the other with me and Grace.

"She's nice," I tell him.

"She's in the wedding?" Joseph's got a cocky smile on his face and it breaks the tension. I let out a laugh as he stands up, taking another drink. "Must be serious if she's *in* the wedding."

Shaking my head, I stare at the back wall, at the unfinished bar. "I'm going to need another beer soon," I mutter to my brother-in-law. It makes him laugh, deep and low, and he relaxes his posture, leaning forward in his seat.

The downstairs would be a good place to hang with him after all.

I need to get down here and finish this room off.

"She's real sweet. A graphic designer." I add the last part absently.

"You met her at the bar?" I look back at my brother-in-law to see his face twisted, and his forehead pinched.

I shove my hands in my pockets and answer, "We hit it off there. It was just friendly at first." I remember way back when I first laid eyes on her.

"That's the way to do it," Joseph comments with a nod and then sucks his teeth. "Friends first."

"Yeah... then I got to missing her." I surprise myself with the omission.

"Yeah I bet." I'm thankful for his simple comment and not looking any deeper into what I just said.

When I bought the bar, Joseph was the only one who backed my decision. Everyone else told me not to pull the trigger, saying it was too risky. That it wasn't a real career. But Joseph was right there. He gave me the pen to sign the papers with. He's a logical man, but in that hairy ass chest of his is a heart of gold.

"So two stable people, two good jobs." Joseph's voice carries a bit.

"We just started seeing each other." Even though my voice is harder than it should be he's unaffected.

He throws his hands up comically. "I'm just saying, you seem happy lately."

I don't get where he's coming from. I didn't pressure him on marriage and babies. Bro code and all. "I'm doing fine."

"Yeah. There's fine, and then there's happy. You're happy."

My lips part to say something back, but I don't know what he wants from me. I just don't want people making a big deal of this and expecting something. It's just fun. For fuck sake, just let us be happy.

"A wife would look good on you."

"You've lost your mind," the words spill out of my mouth.

"You still got that ring?" he asks me. Susanne's ring. An engagement ring I spent all of my savings on. Thinking about it now, half a carat and as simple as they come, there's not much to it. Just like the relationship I had with the woman who wore it.

"No," the lie comes out easy. He snorts, like he knows I'm lying as he tosses his empty beer can into the trash then almost grabs another. But he stops himself. Instead he tells me, "I have to get home."

Finishing the last bit of mine, I toss my beer can in the trash and leave the rest where they are. "I need to get going, too."

The wooden stairs creak as we walk up the rickety steps. When he opens the door at the top, I flick the light switch off and the afternoon daylight filters down the stairway.

Almost time for work. Always working.

That day off with Grace made me realize how much I've been sacrificing. And what I could be doing if I wasn't at the bar all the damn time.

It's not an option yet, but I finally let Maggie go through applications for a manager. The memory of her broad smile and how she shoved my chest in victory makes me huff a short laugh that gets my brother-in-law's attention.

"Let me know if it quits again," Joseph tells me as he heads to the front door, not breaking his stride.

"Will do." With my arms crossed, I stand in the foyer with him as he slips on his boots. "You coming on Sunday?" He missed the last two family dinners. I know he doesn't need anyone nagging him, I'm just curious. I don't hold it against him.

"Yeah, I should be able to. I think we're getting into the flow of things." I can see the hint of relief in his expression.

"Alright then," I comment as he reaches in for a quick hug.

"See you Sunday," he says, turning to leave.

"See you Sunday," I repeat, shoving my hands into my jean pockets and watching him go. My voice is lowered, and I'm not sure if he hears me or not. But it's alright.

Joseph shuts the door behind him, and I head upstairs to grab my wallet and keys so I can get going, too. As I shove the wallet into my back pocket, my eyes flicker to the dresser.

I don't even think about walking over and pulling out the top drawer where the ring is. It just happens.

The small diamond twinkles. It looks brand new, as if my ex never even wore it. The thought makes me happier than it should. I wish I'd never given it to her. I felt obligated to. As I stare at the ring, the memories come flooding back.

I was her first, and her high school sweetheart. Not that there was anything sweet about her. We had some alright moments, but I felt chained to her. After all, everyone knew what we'd done.

They expected us to stay together. They expected all the little boxes to get checked off, and for us to do what we were supposed to. Her cheating on me was one of the best things that could've happened. It gave me an out. A heavy weight lifts off my shoulders as I realize how true that statement is.

And how fucking sad it is, that I would've married her, even knowing I never really loved her. Maybe back then I

139

thought that was what life was supposed to be. But right here and now, no. I didn't love her; not like I know how to love now. She damn sure didn't love me.

As the thought hits me, my phone beeps in my back pocket.

My first thought is that it's Grace. I'm surprised by how disappointed I am when I see it's Cheryl.

Did Joseph leave yet?

My poor sister. All alone with little Miss Evie. I can just imagine her rocking their baby girl while sending this text and listening to her baby girl cry. It's all a phase, but I already know she's going to miss it when Evie's over it. Maybe not the crying, but the wanting to be held. Hell, Joseph may miss it even more.

Just left. I type the message and add, *Love you,* just as she sends back her response.

Thanks. Love you too.

The trace of a smile picks my lips up, but then I see the time. *Shit.* I have to get my ass going. The ring flips back and forth as I roll my fingers over the thin band, making my way out.

There's no way in hell I'm not getting married. My ma would kill me. Just the thought makes my steps down the stairs lighter. I'm not getting any younger. And it's about damn time I had someone in my life. *Someone like Grace.* I don't know if she's the one. My heart flips at the thought of her in a white dress.

I want her, I know that much. But I don't have to know any more than that. She's mine for now, and we're both enjoying ourselves. That's what matters. There's no need to put a label on it.

I grab my jacket off the coatrack and slip on my boots.

She should be at the bar tonight, but she's got a thing with my sister first. A deep chuckle vibrates up my chest. I'm sure she'll have plenty to say about that.

Before I get in the car, I slip the ring in my pocket, knowing the church right up the street has a donation bin. I'm tossing the ring in there before I get to work. I need it gone and out of my life. There's no way I'd give this ring to my wife. All this ring represents is my past. It was meant for Suzanne.

I never wanted her back. That ring was just a reminder of what I was going to end up with.

I'll never settle. As that thought passes through my mind, I realize I should've thrown that damn thing away a long time ago.

Chapter
NINETEEN

Grace

P eeking at my phone again, I read the text from Charlie's sister, Ali. It was sent to all the women in the bridal party.

Let's meet at 1 p.m. at Monique's Bridal! There will be champagne. :)

With a deep breath in I stare out my car window and take in the view, namely Monique's Bridal Shop. It doesn't take long before I see a gaggle of girls come around the corner, and spot Alianna in the middle of them.

A mix of emotions are running through me, but I shove them down and get out of the car, crossing the street toward them with my keys jingling in my hands.

Ali spots me nearly instantly and I keep the smile plastered on my face. "Oh, it's Grace!" She calls out, "I'm so glad you came!"

She hugs me, and it only eases the anxiousness of meeting new people and being in her bridal party – which still makes me feel like I'm crazy for agreeing to do it. She has to be the crazier one though, right? How awful that I'm thinking that as I pull away and wave to the other women who are obviously her friends and far closer to her than I will probably ever be.

"Hi guys," the greeting leaves me and I swallow thickly, trying to shake off every nerve and just enjoy this trip, get to know Ali and have a good time.

I already feel guilty for being on this shopping trip, seeing as how I'm not really dating Charlie. No need to make it weird on top of that by being my... well, weird self. *But they don't know that.*

"I can't tell you how happy I am that you made it!"

"No problem!" I say, trying to make my voice sound upbeat.

"Let me make introductions before we go inside," Ali announces with an excited flare and a quick clap of her hands. "This is Lindsay, Sam, and Ellie."

She gestures to three women. Two of them are petite and blonde like Ali herself, and they're dressed as preppy as J. Crew models. Ellie seems to be the odd one out, tall and thin, dark-haired and wearing an artsy, hot pink dress. Cheryl isn't coming, but she's the last bridesmaid. She texted in the group message that she hadn't slept at all with Evie being up all night.

Altogether, they seem really nice and they're warm to me. So, it's off to a good start!

"Hi," I say. "It's nice to meet y'all."

"Ladies, this is Grace. She's dating Charlie."

I note the looks of total surprise on all three of their faces, followed by a look on Lindsay's face like she smelled something rotten. I assume that look isn't directed at me, but I still saw it.

I guess Diane isn't the only one to have the hots for Charlie.

RIP that good start. At least it lasted a second.

Sam and Ellie say hello, but Lindsay just gives me a tight smile. Luckily, Ali is too caught up in starting the dress shopping to notice. My heart races and the nerves build up even more as she ushers everyone toward the store.

"Come on! Let's go in!" Ali leads the pack, which now I'm a part of.

The window display sports a lady mannequin dressed in what I assume is the height of bridal couture. The dress is white satin, tightly fitted and turned to the side to showcase the low-cut back.

It makes me wonder what kind of dress Ali is looking for, exactly. I don't know a darn thing about her really or about the wedding.

The second we're inside, I pause, waiting for someone to tell us where to go, but we're ushered back and then father back; Ali knows just where to go and doesn't wait for anyone. There's a single podium along the back wall, empty at the moment, and a curved wall that blocks the rest of the store from sight. All the decor is colored in shades of white, cream and pastel pink.

"Hello, hello," a woman appears from a side door right on cue. She speaks clearly, but with a Parisian accent. "You're here for Alianna?" Her elegant demeanor, graying hair and thin frame fit in with the store. This woman looks like she owns the place.

"Yes! That's me," Ali raises her hand while practically shaking with excitement. She's freaking adorable. It warms my heart to see her happiness on such obvious display.

"*Bien*. I'm Monique, the owner. Let me get you ladies set up." There's a large round pink ottoman to sit on, two stuffed chairs, and a *throne*. Like an actual throne. I take it that's going to be for the bride-to-be.

To our left, there's a floor to ceiling three-way mirror with a low pedestal in the middle. Ali looks at the pedestal nervously.

"You sit here," Monique says to Ali, gesturing to the throne. "And the rest of you, sit where you like."

Ali glances at us, her perfect smile never dimming, then goes to sit on the gilded throne. After a minute of being left to our own devices as Monique runs to the back room she came from to grab a client form, Ali grins even wider, I don't know how that's possible. Lindsay and Sam take the two chairs, leaving Ellie and me to sit on the ottoman.

"All right," Monique announces as she enters again with a clipboard and pen. Her English is perfect, though her accent is heavy and honestly adds to the romanticism. "What are we looking for, Miss Alianna?"

Ali turns a pretty shade of pink. "Okay, I already have the reception dress." Her confidence growing as she talks. "My wedding is in a week, and I need a second dress for the ceremony. I wasn't going to do two dresses, but my ma wants something more traditional even though it's a smaller, more casual wedding." I almost laugh at Ali's answer. Charlie told me how his mom has been very opinionated with Ali's dress. I guess she finally gave in one full week before the deadline. She's cutting it close.

"Okay. Tell me what this ideal dress looks like."

"Umm, I brought some pictures…" Ali answers, digging through her purse all the while. The entire place is as quiet as a mouse as we wait. "Here. I made an album of the dresses

145

that I like from the bridal magazines… and the ones my mother liked too."

"Ah!" Monique nods, reaching out. "Let's see."

She takes the stack of photos from Ali and sifts through them. She's quiet for a long time, taking the measure of each picture fully. I wish it wasn't so quiet, it makes me pick at a non-existent piece of lint as my insecurities rise. I don't want to ruin this for Ali. I don't want her to look back on this day and wish I hadn't been there.

"Do you think you'll be able to help us?" Sam asks, fidgety. "She waited until the last minute," she adds, giving Ali a face which only makes Ali give her a face back.

"Of course," Monique responds, very seriously. "I have dresses on hand that will need to be altered, but I promise you, love," she turns her attention from the photos to Ali, "you will fall in love with one of them and so will your mother." The beam of a smile Ali returns and glistening of her eyes forces a wide smile from me too.

"Oh," Sam responds, with a clap not unlike the one Ali had before introductions outside. "Well, alright!"

"Come, come. Let us get you started," Monique says with a smile of her own. "The fitting room is right here. Marcus will be in with some champagne shortly." I don't know who Marcus is, but I could use that champagne. So at the moment, he is my hero in the making.

Ali beams, following Monique to an area behind a heavy pink brocade curtain and leaving us alone. The second, Ali's gone I catch Lindsay looking at me, then she rolls her eyes and leans over to whisper to Sam. My body temperature drops as I look at Ellie, who gives me a sympathetic smile.

"I don't know much about wedding dress shopping," I say, fumbling for something to break the ice.

"Oh, me neither. My sister came here for her wedding dress, though," Ellie talks to me easily. She runs her hand over her dark hair, which is up in a messy bun. "It's nice. Monique is something else."

"Yes this place is beautiful," I agree.

A door opens on the far side of the room, and an older man comes in with a tray of glasses and a bottle of champagne. *Oh, thank goodness.* He doesn't say much other than polite necessities. He simply pours the champagne into flutes and passes them out.

"Thank you," I tell him, accepting the champagne gratefully. It's sweet, and the bubbles tickle my tongue.

"Mmmm," Ellie says. "Thank God for alcohol."

"Yes, I was looking forward to this," I say with a shrug to make my words seem casual. "So how do you know Ali?"

"Ali was my roommate during our first couple of years of college," Ellie says.

"Ahh. I was wondering how you knew each other."

Ellie smiles and sips her champagne. Before I'm forced to think of something else to say, Ali makes her first appearance.

She's stunning, wearing a silky number that has a strappy back, a simple front, and clings to her hips. Oh my goodness. She's a sight to see.

"Oooh, champagne!" she says, rushing to pick up her glass from where Marcus left the tray.

Her sip of champagne comes first and then she makes her way to the mirror, the dress gliding flawlessly. Without even standing on the pedestal, she pans the dress.

"Mmmm, no," she says. "Monique is bringing more options. I just can't see meeting at the altar in this... the straps remind me of like... bondage."

I laugh, a soft feminine laugh. "If you say so. I think you look beautiful."

"It's beautiful," Lindsay says. "Bondage or not."

Ali sweeps over to the ottoman, perching beside me.

"I know all about these bitches," she says, leaning closer to me. "But nothing about you, Grace. Tell me about yourself."

"What do you want to know?" The small bit of tension that left with Ali's joke comes back full force.

"I don't know. Where did you grow up?"

"Here. I'm an Atlanta baby."

"And your family? Big, small?" She asks another easy question.

"Small family. It's just myself and my younger sister, besides my mom."

"Did you go to college?" Ellie asks.

"I did. I went to Brenau University for one year, then I finished my degree at Rhode Island School of Design. I'm a graphic designer now."

"*You* went to RISD?" Lindsay questions from across the room, disbelieving.

"Yeah?" I answer, uncertain. "I studied watercolor and oil painting along with graphic design."

"I went to Savannah College of Art and Design," she says. "I'm an interior designer."

"Oh! That's really cool," I say. *Small world.*

"She's also Charlie's ex-girlfriend," Sam announces, crossing her arms and one perfectly penciled eyebrow lifting.

Ali laughs in a way that shuts down Sam's comment. "No, she *wanted* to be Charlie's girlfriend. There's a huge difference."

I bite my lip, I am really not into this ex-girlfriend, current girlfriend animosity. Ali doesn't seem to catch on to it. Which is good, since this is her day. Marcus was my hero before, this time it's Monique. She pokes her head in to call Ali back. "Alianna, my dear. I have three more dresses for you to try on."

"I'll be back," Ali says, winking to me. "Try not to get into any catfights." The last comment is directed at Lindsay. Maybe Ali did catch on to it.

Without Ali here, the air is somewhat different. Although Ellie asks Sam about some promotion she was wanting to get. Sam didn't hear back yet, but I tell her I hope she gets it. It's only small talk, polite and fairly easy. I don't make eye contact with Charlie's supposed ex though.

It's far too long before Ali makes her way back to us in a new gown, and I deliberately don't look up. I'll just sip my champagne, smile and ooh and ahh when I'm supposed to. Or at least I'll try to.

Ali's hips sway as she walks to the mirror. This one is pretty, but not as formal as the other one. It's sleeveless, dark cream lace with a cutout in the back. Ali's face falls when she sees her reflection in the mirror.

Ali makes her way to the pedestal, turning this way and that. She faces us again. "What do you think?"

"Pretty," Sam pipes up.

"Yeah, pretty," Ellie says, nodding her head as her eyes travel up and down the gown.

"Not pretty enough, though," Lindsay admits. Ali nods, subtly, but still looks to me for my opinion.

"I think I agree," I say. "But it is pretty," I add with a peppy voice just in case she likes it and I was wrong about the facial cues.

"Yeah," Ali agrees, shoulders slumping. "All right. Cheer me up with some more details about yourself. Tell us how you met Charlie."

"Oh, yeah!" Ellie says. "How'd you meet that hunk of

man candy?" Her question forces a grin on my face. When the other girls look at her funny, she shrugs. "What? I can't think that Ali's brother is hot?"

The room fills with snickers.

"Okay," I say, returning my attention back to Ali. "Charlie and I met because my friend Diane told me about his bar. She took me there for a drink, and one thing led to another..."

I leave it open-ended, hoping that their imaginations will be better than mine.

"When are you going to officially be his girlfriend?" Lindsay asks pointedly.

Her question is like a bucket of ice water to the face and I'm sure my expression reflects that. I'm quick to fix it, smiling back at her and shrugging. Before I can manage a response, Ali steps in.

"Charlie said she was. So she is."

"Did he?" her friend questions and even if this conversation wasn't about me, my jaw would still hit the floor. Why would she ruin her friend's big day?

"Jesus, Lindsay," Ali says, getting up. "You really are no fun when it comes to Charlie, you know that?"

"Sorry," Lindsay mumbles and to her credit she does appear remorseful.

With a disapproving look and a huff, Ali disappears into the changing room again before I have to answer. I should try for diplomacy with Lindsay. After all, I'm the one who's full of crap. I know Charlie doesn't want me to really be his girlfriend. If I wasn't in the way, Lindsay could be putting the moves on Charlie. She could be winning his heart, for all I know.

The idea of the pretty little blonde with big handsome Charlie makes me nauseated, but I choke it down, and wash the bad taste out of my mouth with another gulp of champagne. I'm going to play nice with Lindsay.

"I just started dating Charlie," I tell her waving off the tension. "It's barely even a thing."

"Yeah?" she says, looking surprised.

"Yeah, totally. Like, we haven't had any talk about exclusivity or babies or marriage. We've only just started seeing each other." I bite my tongue as soon as I say that. Charlie probably won't appreciate that I've given Lindsay license to kill where he's concerned. It's true though. What's the saying? The truth hurts.

Another gulp of champagne it is.

"Wow. Well… okay," she says, some of her gloom lifting. Although she's now smiling, my heart hurts and I wish I hadn't said that. But I can't take it back now.

I should have said, I really like him and he really likes me. And left it at that.

When Ali arrives again, she makes an entrance. The way she looks in the third dress knocks the breath right out of me. The dress is pure white, with delicate lace straps, lacy cups, and a full skirt. She turns, and the back has a row of tiny white buttons.

There's a collective gasp in the room. She climbs up on the pedestal, straightening her skirts and looks at us in the mirror.

"Y'all," she takes a minute to sway and then says, "I think I found my dress."

"Yay!" Ellie and I clap in unison.

"That is definitely the one," Lindsay affirms, her expression finally resembling happiness for her friend.

"No kidding," Sam says, getting misty-eyed. "You're a gorgeous bride."

"And look!" Ali says, pulling up her skirts to reveal a pair of cowboy boots. "We're all going to wear these under our dresses." I can't help but smile. "Cute, don't you think?" she asks.

"Definitely," Sam nods in agreement.

"You and Charlie can knock boots. Literally," Ali says devilishly.

I blush. "Yeah… maybe."

I laugh, and the other girls smile. Marcus appears to refill our champagne glasses, and I absently empty my glass before he gets to mine, wondering what Charlie would say to that.

Chapter
TWENTY

Charlie

"So your sister's friend Lindsay has the hots for you," Grace lowers her voice to tell me something I already know, leaning against the bar top and taking a small swig of beer. It's late. Really late for her to be out, but I'm glad she's still here. The bar's nearly empty, and closing time is minutes away. Maggie and the others have already left. The drone of the television and one other person are the only things accompanying us. I can't wait to get her alone. Mickey needs to take the hint and get the fuck out of here, but he always stays till I close. I get why he doesn't want to leave though, and so I'm not going to kick him out. He just doesn't want to go home where he's going to be alone and miss his wife.

"Oh she does?" I tease Grace with an asymmetric grin. "I don't really care; I've got the hots for you." I almost said *only* for you, but I'm careful with my words. I want Grace, but I don't want to lead her on. She's made it clear what she wants. I respect that, but I'm a little too addicted to her writhing under me to let her go just yet. Besides the wedding's only a couple of days away. She's all mine till then.

She holds my gaze as she tips her beer back. The baby blues looking for something more from me.

"Come on sweetheart, tell me you've got the hots for me." As I flirt with her, Mickey gets up from his seat and yells out, "Alright, I'm gone." He grabs the remote as if he's at a friend's house, turns off the TV, and tosses it onto the table where it belongs as he walks out.

"Drive safe," I call out to him, leaving my spot at the bar to follow him out and he turns around stopping me with a gesture. He glances at Grace behind me and gives me a look.

"You two have a good night."

A smile curves my lips up as I follow him to the door and open it for him.

The second I lock the door I turn around to see a heat in Grace's gaze. My dick's already hardening watching the way she shifts shyly on the barstool. I love the blush on her. It's only for me.

"Last time I had you in the back room," I lower my voice as I stalk my way to her. "This time I want you on the bar top." Her eyes widen, and her breath hitches, her chest rising higher and falling with her heavy intakes.

"Right here?" she asks, splaying her hands across the bar behind her without breaking our gaze. The way she leans back makes her breasts push forward. She's doing it on purpose and I love it.

"Right fucking there. So every day I come in here I can remember how your back bowed as I fucked you on my bar," I breathe the words into the crook of her neck.

I let my fingers trail down her sides, watching as goose-bumps form down her arms. She's so responsive. I leave an open-mouth kiss just behind her ear, on that sensitive part of her neck and she moans softly in response, almost a whimper.

My fingers dig into the dip in her waist and I wait for her to open her eyes. When she does, her baby blues shine with lust. "Get your ass up here and get naked for me."

There isn't a second that she hesitates. She moves the second I give her the command. She turns her lush ass to me, crawling onto the bar top. The lighting is dim in the bar and this far back, no one will be able to see what we're doing from the front windows.

But I'll know. I'll remember how I had her, long after she's gone.

I'm eager to pull my shirt off and get back to my view of Grace slipping the sleeves of her shirt down her shoulders and stripping out of her clothes as quickly as she can. She's eager too, maybe more so.

My jeans fall into a puddle on the floor and I push my boxers down and step out of them, standing in front of her naked and hard as a fucking rock.

A shuddering breath leaves her as she pushes her clothes off the bar, sitting on her bare ass with her knees bent and her feet on the bar. Her breathing comes in deep as she finds my eyes and licks her lips.

We're both bared to each other, in the same spot we first met. I knew then that I wanted her, but I never thought it'd happen.

A grin stretches across my face at the realization that it really is happening after all.

"Lie down, sweetheart." I climb up on the bar, using the stool as a step and spread her legs. A gentle push on her inner thighs is all I need to get access to her glistening pussy. Fuck. She's so wet. I can't help but to pick her ass up with both hands and tilt her hips so I can easily take a languid lick. A sweet merciful sound is uttered from her lips and it fuels me on.

My blunt nails dig into her flesh as she writhes on the bar. I smile into her heat, tasting her sweetness and feeling conflicted on whether I should get her off this way, or just fuck her hard and rough like I want.

I let go of her with my right hand, to push two fingers into her tight pussy and feel how ready she is. I know I'm a little bigger than she's used to, and I don't want to hurt her.

But I don't want to wait either.

Her sweet moan accompanies her back arching as I curve my fingers and stroke her G-spot. My dick twitches, and a strangled groan vibrates up through my chest. It takes every fucking ounce of effort I have to keep my eyes on her and not let my head fall back when I feel how fucking tight she is. Just the thought of her tight pussy wrapped around my dick is nearly enough to set me off.

She's already close, I know she is. *Come on Grace. Give it to me.*

"You like that?" I question her in a rough breath, kissing her inner thigh afterwards. I never stop stroking her front wall, pressing a bit harder as she stretches for me. Her pussy clenches tighter and her arousal soaks my hand as I push her higher and higher.

Her head thrashes as she breathes the word out. "Yes," she moans and it's barely audible.

I press my thumb to her clit, ruthlessly rubbing circles and her ass jumps in response, her thighs shaking. As she moans my name, I pin her down and I can't move, my body paralyzed from watching the pleasure overtake her body. She's gorgeous like this. She struggles to stay still as I pick up the pace of my movements, desperately needing her to get off.

"Yes!" she screams out, gripping the bar with both hands as her body shakes and her legs try to close tight around me. *Fuck yes*. Her pussy spasms around my fingers and I don't wait for her orgasm to finish. I need her right fucking now.

Climbing between her legs, I spread the bead of pre-cum over the head of my dick and stroke it. Shit! I forgot the condom.

Her one leg wraps around my waist, the heel of her foot digging into my ass. "Charlie, please," she begs me.

"Condom," I barely get the word out, but I don't try to pull away. "Shit, I need a condom." I don't know if I have another.

"No condom," she shakes her head, her heel pushing harder at my ass and that's all I need. "You don't need to if you don't want to. It's not like…" Her voice drifts off and she doesn't have to explain. It's not like I can forget what she told me weeks ago.

Before the sadness can creep any deeper into her heated gaze, I line my dick up between her hot, slick folds and push in gently at first. Just enough so I can lean forward and brace my arms on either side of her head. Her body's so small beneath mine.

Easing in gently, I tilt my hips and rock into her, slowly stretching her. I'm mesmerized by her face the entire time. Her lips part, and her forehead pinches. I'm quick to reach down and put gentle pressure on her clit with slow circles. Her eyes roll back in her head, and her soft moans fill the room. It gets her to relax and I slide in deeper and easier although there's still some resistance.

I can barely breathe with how tight she is. She feels too fucking good.

When her expression turns a little bit more to pain than I want, I wait a minute, kissing her neck and rubbing her throbbing nub before pushing my way back in.

My lips travel up and down her neck, leaving kisses all along the way.

As soon as I'm buried deep inside of her, I pull back to look her in the eyes.

And in that moment, something switches for me. Something changes between us. I don't know what it is, a spark, a pull. Something raw and pure. Something that's scary as all hell that I don't want to face.

I pull back quickly and slam into her, groaning and falling forward as a cold sweat breaks out along every inch of my skin.

I wait, pushing my chest against hers to keep her pinned down as her pussy spasms around my dick. Her body tenses and I give her a moment… and then do it again.

She cries out "yes!" and I don't wait this time. She's hot, wet and ready for me to fuck her pretty little pussy the way she deserves to be fucked. I angle my hips so each time I thrust all the way to the hilt, my groin smacking against her clit.

"Charlie," she mewls, her hands flying to my shoulders and her nails digging into my skin as I piston my hips, taking her rough and hard. And raw.

Fuck, she feels so good. I bury my head in the crook of her neck, feeling my hot breath against her heated skin. I don't stop, I don't let up my pace.

I'm so fucking close though. My balls draw up, and my spine tingles. I hold my breath, needing her to come with me. A sweat breaks out along my skin as I pump my hips faster.

I need her to get off with me. And just as I'm about to lose it, she ignites under me. A cry of pleasure leaves her lips and her nails scratch down my back.

I thrust my hips in shallow pumps until I come, still deep inside of her. My release washes through me in waves. And I finally breathe, taking in her sweet scent as my dick pulses and I empty myself inside of her.

I finally lift my head up to look at her. And that spark, that pull is even stronger.

Her head lolls to the side as we both catch our breath.

Swallowing thickly, I gently pull out of her. My heart races, and it won't quit.

Something happened. Something changed.

But I ignore it as I climb down and reach for the paper towels under the bar. She doesn't look me in the eyes as I wipe between her legs.

All I want to know is if she felt it, too.

Chapter
TWENTY-ONE
Grace

Everything's crazy, but in the hushed, well-heeled way that only weddings can be. It's the day of the wedding, and I'm right in the thick of it.

The suite of rooms reserved for the bride to get ready in are packed with her bridal party and makeup artist and planner. It's a production to say the least and I'm doing my part sitting in my spot, complete with a name tag and getting my makeup and hair finished by two aestheticians. One lady sweeps a bit of blush on my cheeks. The other lady puts a final pin in my hair, backing away to stare at me as she considers her work.

Given that it's summer the sun is still up and bright, shining through the large open windows even though it's nearly 6 p.m. I'm the last one of the girls to be made up and the others are having pictures taken.

"I think you're finished," the hairstylist announces behind me.

I squirm in my seat. The two ladies wouldn't let me look while they were doing my hair and makeup. They wanted to surprise me but promised I'd love it. I'm not used to being pampered like this. It's nice though. Apart from all the nerves and rushed women and men coming in and out to update the bride, it's been amazing.

"Okay," the hair stylist says. "I'm done."

"Me too," the makeup artist says, setting her brushes to the side and backing away. "You can go look now."

I'm a bundle of nerves as I walk to the bathroom. When I peer in the mirror; a dewier, much more polished version of myself looks back at me. My hair is braided and pinned up. My makeup is a little more extravagant than I usually go with. My lashes... my goodness! I love them long like this. I wonder what Charlie will think.

I run my fingers down the length of my dress, which is the ocean blue silk with triangular side cutouts I bought before I knew I'd be in the party. I twirl a bit feeling giddy, and smile at the way the floor-length gown moves.

"Grace!" Ellie calls and snaps me out of my little fantasy. Today isn't my day. It's Ali's. "In here!" I call out but she's already in the doorway.

"You look so pretty," she comments with a smile that widens. I match it and tell her she looks gorgeous too.

"Love your dress," I add and with my comment she does a half swirl with her skirt.

"It's so funny how each of our dresses are different but they go together. These pictures are going to be A-ma-zing." She emphasizes.

I can only nod, not trusting myself to speak. Sleep evaded

me last night, knowing that after today, Charlie and I are probably going to be done with. It's just for fun. That's all it ever was. The pictures are just a reminder that I lied to his sister and mother.

I feel like a fraud taking part in this moment. As much as I feel bad for Ali, having some soon-to-be stranger in her photos, I feel more sickly knowing once tonight is done, the charade is over. I think Charlie would let it continue a while. But I can't keep doing this, pretending like this is okay. It's not just fun for me. Not anymore. I'm falling for him… hard. And I'm only going to end up hurt.

"The bridesmaids are all meeting downstairs for pre-wedding toasts."

"Oh! Okay. Let me get my boots, and I'll be right down. Don't wait for me. I don't want to hold anything up." Where the hell did I leave those boots? The suite is littered with purses and makeup bags and all sorts of wedding paraphernalia.

Elli gives me a quick, "be fast" heading out of the room with the other girls. I make sure to thank the makeup artist and hair stylist, then hunt for my boots which are our wedding gift from Ali.

I check the shoe rack in the closet. They're the only pair left. I'm careful sitting down on the bed not to mess my dress up so I can pull the boots on. The leather is fresh; the boots still brand new.

Who'd have guessed that the shine on my boots would last longer than my relationship with Charlie? Without sleep and all of these people around me who I've lied to, my insecurities are on full blast.

Anyone with eyes could've seen that coming, I tell myself. My throat feels tight as I stand up and hightail it downstairs. Exiting the elevator, I pick up my dress to keep it from dragging as I search for the girls, making my way to the hotel lobby. I pass the ballroom, where the reception will take place. It's gorgeous. Mostly white and cream with pops of blue hydrangeas and blue glassware. Utterly magazine worthy. After checking a couple of empty rooms, I find the girls drinking from a silver flask in what seems to be a coat closet.

"Hey!" Sam says, eyes twinkling. "We were just warming up."

"I see that," I say, smiling. "Is it my turn?"

Lindsay hands the flask to me, and I take a swig. I wince; it's bourbon.

"Wow. Strong," I wheeze. Oh my goodness I was not prepared for that.

I pass the flask on to Ali. She looks at it, considering, then shakes her head. "No more for me." She passes the flask and then shakes out her hands. "The adrenaline is in full swing and I can barely feel the last two shots but I know they'll hit me."

"You think the guys are drinking?" Ellie asks.

"The groomsmen definitely are. I saw Chris sneaking a whole bottle of whiskey into their suite earlier," Sam confirms with a nod and then another short swig.

"I swear, Michael had better not be falling down drunk," Ali frets, smoothing her hands over her dress.

"Charlie won't let him drink too much," I console her without thinking. As if I know whether or not Charlie would stop his soon to be brother-in-law from drinking on his wedding. I've never even met Michael.

I'm mostly assuaging Ali's fears; I have no idea what Charlie will or won't do.

"Ladies?" the wedding planner asks, poking his head in. "The guests are all seated out on the terrace. They're ready for you all to line up now."

"Oh God," Ali says, gripping Lindsay's hand. "Oh God."

Lindsay passes the flask to Sam, then gives Ali a mini pep talk, getting down on her knees in front of Ali.

"You are ready," she says in a hushed voice. "All you have to do is walk down that aisle, and Michael will be there waiting. You love each other and that's all that matters. That's it."

Ali nods at Lindsay, and I can feel the emotion rolling off of her. Her anxiety and nerves are contagious as I look into her eyes. "I'm really getting married," she whispers and the girls nod. I don't know why I'm all teary eyed. After a moment she whispers, "All right. Let's go."

Chapter
TWENTY-TWO

Charlie

I t's too warm to be wearing this suit. Evening summer weddings are a thing down here. But it's still too hot for suits. Looking forward to the moment the ceremony is over, I pull at my collar a bit, loosening my tie just enough so I can breathe. This jacket is getting ditched the second I can take it off. Michael's to my left, and he looks even worse off than I feel. He clenches and unclenches his hands, shaking them out and shifting his feet.

Ma's in the front row, and she's already crying. She glances at each of us and then back down the aisle like she's done for the last three minutes. It's a few minutes past six thirty. It's time for this thing to get started.

Nearly everyone has eyes on the groom or the card in their hand that they're using to fan themselves. But Michael doesn't even seem to notice. His eyes are focused only on the double doors to the venue, waiting for my sister to walk out in her dress.

I lean in and speak to him out of the side of my mouth, hands still clasped in front of me while we wait. "She's always late; it's not you."

He finally tears his eyes from the doors as Chris, one of his good friends and another groomsman, laughs behind me.

"No, it's definitely you," Chris says, not even trying to stay quiet. A smile kicks my lips up as Michael wipes his hands off on his pants.

He's already back to looking at the doors, not a word in response. The poor guy. My sister's really got him worked up.

"She loves you." I don't know why the words slip out. He knows it. Everyone does. He and Ali were meant to be together.

With a slight asymmetric smile, he relaxes a touch and looks back at me, the worry and nerves still there as he nods his head. "I love her too." The crowd stirs at the sound of an acoustic guitar playing a soft song as the doors finally open.

Here we go; I straighten my back and watch as the first bridesmaid walks out.

My sweetheart. She's breathtaking. The thin dress swishes as she walks down the aisle of pale blue and white petals. My heart thumps and then seems to stop before madly racing, refusing to stay where it's supposed to be.

Her steps are measured and her hands are wrapped around the bouquet of white roses, blue hydrangea and baby's breath. I stare at her, my heart beating slower as she comes closer and everything else blurs around her. She's not walking to me, and she's not the bride, but just the sight of her makes my heart misbehave.

She tucks a bit of hair behind her ear as she takes a

quick peek at the guests. Her nerves can't hide with her head slightly ducked, and it looks so damn good on her.

She's sweet like that. Real sweet.

I can't stop staring at her, willing her to look back at me.

"You're drooling," Chris says, nudging me in the shoulder and I turn to look at him, my hand instinctively going to my mouth.

The guys laugh, including Michael. Jackass. I turn back to her just as she finally makes it to us and catch her stare.

She gives me a sweet, soft smile, complete with a deeper blush on her cheeks, and quickly looks away. My chest fills with warmth, but then she's gone, standing on the other side of Michael and out of my view.

The other bridesmaids file in and then the music changes as my sister appears in the double doors, cueing the crowd to stand and the music to change.

I take the moment while everyone's looking at the bride to peek behind Michael at Grace.

The mask she was wearing is down, and in its place is a look I didn't expect to see. Worry, anxiety. Her eyes though, those beautiful doe eyes are wide with something else.

She must feel my eyes on her, because she turns her head to me and the mask goes right up. Her eyes are still glassy. She can't hide that.

"You okay?" I mouth the question to her.

She nods back and gives me a tight smile. I don't have time to ask her anything else. The wedding's in full swing with the delicate version of the wedding march from the acoustic guitar.

I stand straight and look forward, watching as my father gives Ali away and Michael steps forward. With both hands still clasped in front of me, I get another view of Grace and the sweet facade is back, but I can't forget what I saw.

A tear slips down her cheek and she wipes it quickly, playing it off as if it's the wedding and emotional tears of joy.

But I know better. She may say she's okay. She may play it off.

But I know Grace.

And she's not okay. All I can think is: *what the hell did I do and how do I make this right? Right fucking now.*

Chapter
TWENTY-THREE

Grace

The bar is the best place to be at wedding receptions, and I have no intention of leaving it if I can help it. It's in the back of the ballroom, and the lights have been turned down. The music has gone from upbeat party music to sexy slow jams.

I look down at my glass only to find it empty. *Again.*

All right, maybe I'm a little tipsy. Whoever made the punch wasn't screwing around.

It's been a busy day of meeting people left and right and having to play the part of Charlie's girlfriend. There hasn't been a moment when the two of us have been alone but for the past hour, I've been here, avoiding any contact and trying to convince myself that I'm not a bad person. I didn't want to hurt anyone so it's not wrong, right? It's not bad of me to be in this wedding when I know I'm out of the picture probably hours from now. Wiping a tear from under my eyes before anyone can catch on, I sniffle and pull my shit together. That's when I look up and see Charlie heading my way. Not just my way; he's making a beeline for me.

I take a moment to soak in his large frame, the way his muscles bunch under his white dress shirt as he moves and breathe in deep, calming myself. When he draws closer, I appreciate the clean line of his jaw, the intense green of his eyes.

"Dance with me," he doesn't mince words, giving me a charming smile.

I give him half a smile back. "You know I've got two left feet, right?" The last thing I want to do right now is dance.

"Just come with me." My heart clenches as he puts his hand out, and I can't help but to slip my hand into his. How could I ever say no to him?

He squeezes my hand, dragging me out to the dance floor. I hate myself for it, but a feeling of intense completion runs through me when his hand wraps around mine. A chill runs down my spine as he turns me, and takes me in his arms; my breath hitching as my boot heels click on the dance floor. My heart is beating faster now.

We start to move to the slow, sultry rhythm. He surprises me, because he's light on his feet. My arms around his neck feel hot, and I wonder if he notices. Or if it's just me.

"I didn't know you could dance," I say.

"There's a lot you don't know about me."

He looks down at me, and I struggle not to drown in the moss green of his eyes.

"Yeah?" I say, to distract myself.

"Mmmhm," he murmurs.

I lean into him a little and I hate that I'm doing it, but it's a memory I get to keep. The heat of his body, his hard chest and masculine smell. I take it all in, closing my eyes and letting out a small sigh.

"Charlie?" I whisper against his chest.

"Yeah?" I feel the rumble of his answer against my cheek.

"Why are you still single?" I ask, our bodies still swaying to the gentle music. "I've seen the type of girls that hang on you. It doesn't make any sense that you haven't picked one of them to date by now."

He's silent for a long time, long enough to make me open my eyes. I stare up at him, hoping I don't look as enraptured as I feel.

This right here, this foolish feeling, is why I've been avoiding him all night. I feel like I need to hold on to him, but I know I can't.

"Are you going to answer?" I ask.

He smiles, but it's forced. "Yeah. I just… it's complicated, you know?"

"So make it simple. Simple enough for me to understand, anyway. I had a few glasses of that punch." I try to lighten up the conversation, but his expression doesn't change.

"Well… I have an ex. A girl named Susanne."

"Oh?" My heart thuds in my chest. I don't want to think about him with someone else.

"She was my high school sweetheart. When I was twenty, I gave her everything I had. I proposed to her with the biggest diamond I could get, which granted wasn't very large. I was twenty, after all."

"Wait, you were married?" I say, pulling back.

"No. Engaged," he says, pulling me back into his arms. "And not engaged for long. About a month later, I walked in on her with someone else."

"You didn't!" I freeze where we're standing, my eyes large

171

as the shock runs through me. Who the hell would cheat on him? She must've lost her damn mind.

"I did." He nods his head and moves me on the dance floor, willing me to keep dancing with him and I relent. I won't deny him. My poor Charlie. Some dumb girl broke his heart and I hate her for it.

"I'm sorry," I say, squeezing him gently and trying to settle into his arms again. I can vaguely feel and hear everyone around us, but my thoughts are only on him.

"Well, it worked out. The next year, I got a job at a bar. Saved up all my money, worked a ton. Bought Mac's the second he tried to sell it."

"And the fiancée?"

"Haven't seen her since. She moved out of town not long after."

I lay my head against his chest for a minute, thinking about how he must've felt. No wonder he doesn't want commitment. My voice cracks and I have to clear my throat to tell him, "You know, not all women are like that. Not every woman will break your heart."

He shrugs, his shirt moving gently against my nose as I stay pinned to his chest. "Sure."

"Sure isn't really the kind of answer..." I stop my comment. I don't know how to make this better but I want to.

He looks down at me, perhaps sensing my earnestness. His eyes trail down to my lips, showing just what's on his mind.

I close my eyes and offer up my mouth. Charlie kisses me, tender at first, but then with more passion, making my heart race.

I break off the kiss as I become more fully aware that we're surrounded by other people. "Charlie..."

"We don't need to talk about my past, sweetheart," he whispers, cupping my jaw with a hand.

He kisses me again. I can feel people looking at us. Charlie's family is getting a hell of a show. Still, when he touches me, I feel alive, vibrant. I feel loved and it's not fair. It's not fair because now more than ever I don't think Charlie will ever give his heart away. Not to me. But he has mine and it hurts for us.

I groan quietly when Charlie breaks away to kiss my neck. Lightning bolts shoot through my body at the touch of his lips against my skin.

Then he leans down to whisper in my ear. "Come with me..."

He takes my hand and leads me from the dance floor.

Chapter
TWENTY-FOUR

Charlie

Subtle doesn't suit me but I try to be as subtle as possible as I weave through the family and friends in the ballroom, dragging Grace behind me. She's holding onto my hand with both of hers, just trying to keep up.

I smile at my aunt sitting at a table close to the dance floor, and give her a small wave, pretending not to see her gesture me over to talk to her.

Grace needs me right now, and I'm not stopping until she's better.

Specifically, until I get her off and make damn sure she knows she's mine and I'm hers.

The music and loud sounds of the ballroom fade as I lead Grace through the double doors and down the hallway. Out here, she pulls herself closer to me and I slow my steps to wrap my arm around her waist, looking for somewhere to go for a bit of privacy.

"Where are we going?" Grace asks, her curves pressing against my body as she looks at me with those beautiful doe eyes full of questions.

I catch sight of the coat check down the hall and to the right, and a wicked smile curves my lips up.

Lowering my head to her ear, I whisper, "I need to take care of you."

I don't wait for her to respond. She nearly stumbles, although she lets out a small laugh when she does, as I pull her along, opening the half door and walking away from the counter and to the back where there are rows and rows of coats.

"What in the hell?" she says, but her voice is playful. The smile on her face is genuine and I love it. That's the smile that should have been with her all damn day. With one foot after the other, I walk her backwards in between the two rows of coats and all the way to the back. The light's obstructed from the hanging linens, so it's dim, but I can still see the blush on her cheeks.

"Charlie, you are crazy if you think-" I cut her off, pressing my lips against hers and cupping the back of her head. She doesn't protest, but instead parts her lips and lets me in.

Deepening the kiss, my tongue strokes against hers as our warm breaths mingle. And when I break the kiss, she's breathless, the fight in her gone.

"Crazy if what?" I ask her, daring her to give me that lip of hers.

She sags against the wall, breathing heavy, her lips still parted. "To think I'm going to let you…" she trails off and licks her lips.

"Let me what?" I lean closer to her, resting my forehead on hers and staring into her eyes, "Let me get you off?"

Her eyes spark, and she doesn't answer.

I crouch down, grabbing the hem of her dress, and then slowly stand, pulling it up. She holds my gaze as I hitch it around her hips.

"You wet right now?" I murmur the question. She bites her lip, and her eyes dart behind me. If my hand wasn't inches away from her, I bet she'd lie to me.

My fingertips gently touch the seams to her panties. I don't feel enough of her heat, so I push them aside, holding those blue eyes to mine and gently pushing my fingers into her hot entrance.

She's soaking wet.

She visibly swallows, her head falling back against the wall, as I brush my fingers up to her clit, moving the moisture there.

"You think it'd be crazy?" I ask her.

She licks her lips, her breathing picking up and then shakes her head no.

I narrow my eyes and lean forward, "Tell me what you want, sweetheart."

Even without much light, I catch sight of her blush and then she looks away. I wait for her. Letting her choose this. Letting her choose me.

My fingers trail back down to her entrance and back up to her clit, a shudder running through her body.

"Please," she moans into the air, her back bowing as she tries to grind her pussy into my hand. I smile down at her. "Please what?"

"Please…" she hesitates to answer as her eyes dart behind me again. I look over my shoulder, but no one's there.

"I'm not going to let anyone see," I tell her firmly. If that's what she's scared about, we'll be alright. We're far enough away that no one's going to catch us and if they come back here, I'll be blocking their view.

Her blue eyes flick to mine. "Please get me off."

My dick turns to stone at her asking me that. I can feel my zipper against my dick and I'm desperate to readjust it, but I can't move my hand away from her pussy.

"Anything for you," I tell her in an even, sincere tone. How it's not strained, I don't know.

"Mmm," she moans softly, closing her eyes as I push my fingers deep inside of her. I push them in and out, loving her warmth and the way she greedily rocks her hips, wanting more. I turn to look over my shoulder once more, just to make sure we're alone.

When I look back at her, her eyes are on me, her head lazily resting against the wall. Her body sways as I pump faster, brushing against her sensitive bundle of nerves each time, making her breathing come faster as she loses her composure.

"I think it would be unbelievable for us to break up right after the wedding," I whisper into her ear, taking her off guard. I'm not a fucking idiot. That has to be what's going through her worried mind. I need to convince her to stay... just a little longer. I don't know if I'll ever get my fill of her, but I'm not going to let her walk away the second she has a chance.

She moans, her eyes going half-lidded. I know she can hear me.

I grind the palm of my hand against her clit. "You should stay with me a little longer." Her breathing comes in frantically as I pick up the pace. She's close, so close. I'm not letting her get off until she agrees though.

Her neck lolls to the side, her cheek pressed against the cold wall as I slip my fingers into her hot pussy and stroke that bundle of nerves. Her eyes pop open, and she covers her mouth with her hand.

"Tell me you'll come by the bar and keep up appearances." I don't know how I get the words out as I work her pussy.

Her head whips back and slams against the wall. "Yes," she calls out as softly as she can, given her current state, and I almost think it's from getting off, but she's not there yet. I pause my movements and she turns her head to look at me, her hands moving to my wrist with a desperate look on her face.

"Yes, what?" I ask her.

She swallows thickly and answers in a whisper, "I'll stay with you-"

I cut her off with a demanding kiss before she says anything else and pump my fingers into her pussy. My palm goes flat against her clit, still over her panties that are pushed to the side. I'm ruthless and rough as she clings to me. She looks paralyzed as her mouth opens and closes and she desperately tries not to cry out.

The moment she comes, her body goes still, tensing as her pussy tightens and her breath hitches. I kiss her neck, still stroking my fingers against her front wall to make her pleasure last. It's only when her body finally sags against the wall that I pull my fingers out of her.

I let her dress fall around her trembling thighs, but I'm not done with her. I didn't intend to fuck her just yet, but the sight of her coming undone from my touch is making me go crazy.

I need her just as much as she needs me.

"I'm gonna fuck you, and you're going to be quiet." I stare into her eyes, willing her to agree. Her eyes dart to the entrance behind us as she licks her lips and her legs scissor. I know this turns her on just as much as it does me. She holds

178

my gaze and then nods, her lips turning up into a devilish smile.

"A quickie?" she asks and it makes me laugh, low and rough.

"If that's what you want to call it," I tell her, reaching for my back pocket out of instinct.

It's only then that I realize I don't have a condom.

For a second, a split second, the idea of knocking her up comes to mind. Pretending it's an accident. She says she can't get pregnant, but fuck that, I can at least try my damnedest.

The thought of her swollen with my baby and tied to me only makes my dick harder. I don't break eye contact as I unzip my pants and shove them down to fall around my ankles.

"Turn around," I give her the command and she doesn't object, still lost in the pleasure I gave her. I hike her dress up, letting my fingers trail along her soft skin and then pull her panties down. I don't miss how damp they are from her getting off.

I take a moment to look at her tight ass and cup her pussy. She's so hot and wet. So ready for me. She's always ready for me.

Bracing a hand on the wall next to her, I push my dick between her folds, feeling her tight walls wrapping around my dick and pulling me in. *Fuck.* She feels like heaven. As I let my forehead fall to the back of her neck, groaning from how good she feels, her hand splays on top of mine and then grips me. I have to open my eyes and pull back to kiss her. But I'm struck by the expression on her face. It's a look of utter rapture.

I move slowly, deeper, filling her inch by inch. And the deeper I go, the more her lips part until they make a perfect "O" when I'm buried deep inside of her.

This is how she should always be. Lost in pleasure.

I don't waste any time. We've already been gone too long for our absence to go unnoticed. I pull back slightly, just a few inches and then fuck her pussy so hard and rough that she cries out.

I'm quick to silence her, turning her head to me and pressing my lips to hers. I pull back, but leave my face close to hers, our warm breath combining and heating with the intensity I feel between us.

She moans my name as her head thrashes.

I slam my dick into her, all the way to the hilt, feeling her lush ass jiggle as I pump my hips over and over again. My breathing comes in frantically as I feel her tighten around my length. *Yes! Come for me again.* I need to feel her get off and watch her as she's consumed with pleasure.

Leaning in closer to her, I whisper in her ear, "Give it to me," and thrust into her again. Her body jolts against the wall as her face scrunches and her mouth parts with a small gasp. "Come for me," I breathe against her slender neck, her body shuddering with a chill and then I bury myself deep inside of her.

Her eyes open as her pussy flutters and her fingernails dig into my hand. She lets out a silent scream, her head falling back against my shoulder as her orgasm rips through her.

It's all I needed. I race for my own release, pistoning my hips and riding through her pleasure. A rough groan low in my throat leaves me as I pound into her tight pussy over and over until a wave of pleasure rocks through me, curling my toes and leaving me out of breath. My dick pulses as I shove myself as deep as I can inside of her, nearly picking her up off the floor.

She whimpers, and I open my eyes as thick spurts of cum fill her, but there's only pleasure on her face.

I want to keep her, so I'll give her what she wants. I have the hotel room tonight with her and I'll do everything I can. Something to tie her to me. She never told me what she wanted from this drunken deal. But I can give her something I know she's after.

A baby.

Chapter
TWENTY-FIVE

Grace

I t's quiet in the area at work as I sit by myself, my head in the clouds. I'm peeling a tangerine, but not really paying any attention to it.

My mind is on Charlie. More specifically, on the deal we had. I fulfilled my end, playing Charlie's pretty girlfriend. And Charlie...

Well, let's just say that his end of the bargain was met when he made me orgasm three times in a row. A blush hits my cheeks just thinking about it. That man does things to me. I've completely fallen for him. Even though I know I shouldn't have, I can't bring myself to regret it.

A piece of the tangerine finds its way into my mouth as I stare absently at some poster on the wall.

So I guess that since we've both held up our ends of the bargain, it's over even though he did ask me to stay a little longer for appearances. I don't want to play games anymore, and that's all this is to him. It's fun and a good time. I agree with all that. But if that's all this is, I need to salvage what's left of my heart.

Showing up at the bar, waiting for him to call it quits is just torture. He's just stringing me along. I sit back and sigh. I don't want it to be over. I want anything but that, really. I want a commitment. I want *more* with him.

And that's my fault.

Facing him and asking for more is only going to leave me alone and brokenhearted even sooner. So my choices are:

1. Rip that band aid off, asking for more and having him end it like I know he will.
2. I can play along for a little while, but that only makes me more pathetic and it's only going to hurt that much worse.

As I stand up, rolling my eyes, I throw the peel of the tangerine in the trash and shove each section in one by one.

Sarah, my immediate boss, sticks her head in the break room. She's redheaded like me and big-boned, but she always dresses like she's on an Italian runway. In short, she's gorgeous. Today she's wearing a black boat neck dress that looks like it cost a million dollars from the way it flatters her frame.

"Hey, Grace." She's cheery as always as she steps into the room.

"Hey," I greet her with a forced smile. I shouldn't feel bad for my afternoon break, everyone takes them. Still, I feel the need to defend myself. "I'm just on my way back to work."

"Do you have a minute? Jack and I would like to talk to you in his office."

I stare at her. Jack Holt is one of the partners at our firm. I've literally only talked to him at Christmas, when he's handing out holiday bonus checks. My heartbeat picks up with anxiety at the thought of having a meeting with him.

I rack my brain to figure out what he could possibly want to talk to me about. A new project? But no, he isn't usually involved on that level.

This is looking really, really bad. I swallow the lump in my throat, searching Sarah's face for a clue, but there's nothing there.

"Uhh… sure." My forced smile falls but I do my best to keep it in place.

"It's nothing bad. Stop looking like I'm taking you to see the grim reaper," Sarah jokes and I laugh in return but only because it's obligatory. "Come on."

Does being fired count as bad? I wonder, trying to calm down. The last of my tangerine gets tossed in the trash and I follow Sarah across the main room where everybody works. Unlike me, most of the employees don't put their heads down while they work, so a few eyes follow me across the room. I glimpse Diane trying to make eye contact with me, but I avoid it. I haven't talked to her since the wedding… *which she didn't attend.*

Sarah leads me to a corner office, where she pauses to knock on the door. I fidget, wiping my hands off on my shirt and trying to stay calm. Sarah wouldn't lie to me.

"Come in," Jack calls through the door and we enter, my legs feeling like jello. Sarah shuts the door behind me, increasing my paranoia that I'm about to be fired.

"Grace, hi," Jack says, standing up from behind his large espresso desk that's littered with paperwork. He's in his fifties, well dressed, and tanned as a nut from long days on his yacht. "Please sit," he gestures to one of two chairs in front of his desk.

I glance at Sarah and pick a chair. Sarah sits in the other one, crossing her legs and smiling. Jack settles himself back behind his desk, looking serious.

My heart thumps wildly. I've never been fired before. My hands are clammy and I try to think of something to say, but I don't trust my voice.

"So Grace, I asked Sarah to recommend someone to run the project desk, keep the designers on task and make sure what they produce is in line with the clients' branding. She recommended you."

Blinking several times, all of them a little too fast, I stare at my boss for a second, processing his words, then look at Sarah. "She did?"

"Apparently you... let's see here," he says, picking up a piece of paper off his desk. He starts to read. "Quote - She works ten times harder than anyone else. If everyone was as dedicated to customer satisfaction and producing great artwork, we would be far more successful. You seem to have an eye for branding not just design." The paper falls with a flutter as he adds, "There's a critical difference and not everyone has it."

"I... I don't know what to say," I manage, my throat feeling dry but in a good way. I manage to answer Jack, although my throat feels tight. "Thank you for noticing."

"Don't thank me. Thank Sarah," Jack says. "Now the promotion comes with a big bump in pay, but ten people working directly below you. You'll be overseeing campaigns and critiquing. You also get final say and can modify and mold designs how you see fit. Can you handle that?"

"I... yes," I say, nodding vigorously. "Absolutely I can." Oh my gosh. I didn't even consider a promotion. A bonus yes, a raise in pay, heck yes, I'll take that any day.

"Alright! Well, Sarah will see that the contract is on your desk by Monday to sign. Thank you for your hard work," Jack says, standing and offering me a handshake.

With the meeting apparently over, I stand and shake his hand, trying not to let him see that I'm trembling. It's an excited tremble. Sarah smiles at me on the way out. I don't know how I'm even walking, I'm so stunned. Once the door is closed behind us, I let out a breath.

"I can't say thank you enough," I confess to Sarah.

She laughs. "I told you it was nothing bad!"

I reach out and almost grab her hand or hug her, but instead I clasp mine in front of me, feeling so grateful and overwhelmed. *Remain professional*, I remind myself. "Thanks so much, Sarah. Really."

"Well, I just wanted you to realize that I see how hard you work. I see all the nights you're here late, and all the crap you put up with from the clients."

"You won't regret this. I promise," I say. The giddiness takes over as the shock wears off.

"I'm sure I won't," she states matter of factly, winking.

We part ways, Sarah back to her office and me back to my cubicle. Still smiling so hard that it hurts, I return to my seat. Immediately, Diane's head pops up over the cubicle walls. Holy shit. I let out a small laugh, short and full of relief.

"You scared the crap out of me," I joke.

"What was that all about?" she asks. "It looked serious."

"I... I actually got a promotion," I admit to her, my smile never waning. "It's weird to say it out loud." Oh my gosh, I got a promotion. It's my first ever. I'm still in disbelief.

"What?" she asks, standing straighter. "Promotion to what?"

"They need someone to manage the project desk," I

answer her, turning in my chair to face her fully and finally breathing normally.

"No way! I thought Melanie was going to run the project desk."

She looks and sounds… pissed. It takes a second to realize that. She's not at all happy for me. The deep crease in the center of her forehead and scowl on her face give that away. She can't even pretend to be happy for me? I swallow, feeling the high die down and answer her, "Well, apparently not. They just offered it to me."

"Congrats! Seriously, that's awesome." Although her words are kind… and rushed, her expression and tone are still off.

"Thanks." I smile and try to shrug it off.

"We should go celebrate later! Go out, grab some drinks." Her fun side comes back, and for a second I think I imagined her original reaction.

I must have. She may be obnoxious at times, but I think about it, then decide what the hell.

"Sure. Maybe we could go to that bar with the awesome Mexican food?" I offer.

"Sarita's? Yeah, girl. And then we can make our way to Mac's."

I go silent, but nod. Charlie said he wants me to come to keep up appearances, but I don't know if I can bring myself to do it. I don't want to get hurt. I don't want to play games anymore.

"What?" Diane asks. "You don't want to go to Mac's?"

"I was just thinking somewhere else would be nice to let loose," I answer her, but even to me it sounds like a lie. My heart hurts just thinking about it.

"Is it because of Charlie? Oh my God, did you two break up?"

"Jesus, Diane!" I say, lowering my voice and looking around. "Not everything is about Charlie."

"You did! You totally broke up," Diane says, a hint of glee evident in her eyes.

"For your information, there was nothing to break up. We were having fun. Leave it alone Diane." I wish I could reach out and snatch my words back. It hurts to say it out loud.

"Were?" she questions and I've had it.

"I said leave it alone." My tone reflects my anger.

"Oh," she says. It's hard to read what she's really thinking. "Well, alright. Let's go to the bar with the Mexican food, then."

"Fine," I say, on edge. I'd rather be angry than anything else. So I cling to that emotion although I think I'm only angry at myself. "I have a lot of work I need to finish first."

"I guess that's why you got the promotion," she says, with a tight smile. "I'll be back at six to bug you, though."

She disappears behind her side of the wall. I'm left trying to decide if I should feel bad for snapping at her.

I slip on my headphones and sink into my work, refusing to think about any of this mess of a love life anymore. Well I try. But that doesn't work. All I can think about is Charlie and how Diane is right. We're over. Break up, labels or whatever. It's over.

Chapter
TWENTY-SIX

Charlie

I'm about two seconds away from texting Grace when she walks through the front door of the bar. *About fucking time.*

I haven't seen her since yesterday morning, the morning after the wedding.

She's still in her work clothes, but her hair is down and swishing around her shoulders as she walks in.

A feminine screech echoes through the bar behind her, and Grace turns to look over her shoulder.

"We're finally here!" Diane's with her, and my expression falls. I don't understand how the two of them are friends. I stay behind the bar and move to the far left, where Grace usually sits and where the dishwasher is. My eyes flicker up and I watch the two of them as I get to work. Diane stumbles slightly and talks a bit too loud. A few customers turn to watch them walk in, but then they go right back to what they were doing before.

"I love this place," Diane says, dragging Grace by the hand. Grace lets her, tucking a strand of hair behind her ear and seemingly not wanting to come over to me. I don't like it, and I don't understand it in the least.

Diane's quick to sit on the barstool at the far end. Grace's stool.

I don't pay her any attention, waiting for Grace to look at me. When she finally does, I can see the same worry there that was on her face at the wedding before she looks away again. That sick feeling of anxiety washes through me. What the hell do I need to do to make her happy?

Make it official.

I grab a glass and wipe it down with a drying cloth as Grace takes a seat.

"Hey there," I speak up, waiting for her gaze to meet mine.

"Hey," her voice is soft. She desperately needs more. She needs a title: girlfriend. For real. My body heats at the thought, but if that's what it takes, I'll give it to her. I'll make it real and let the world know. Ever since the wedding, they've all been pushing me anyway.

I open my mouth to say something to put her at ease, but Diane speaks up, leaning forward and tapping the bar.

"We're getting wasted tonight," she says, already far more drunk than Grace. I cock a brow at her.

"Is that so?" My eyes dart back to Grace as she sets her purse down on the bar.

"Can we have two drink specials, please?" Diane asks, taking my attention again.

"That what you want, sweetheart?" I ask Grace. I hold

those doe eyes when she finally looks back at me. "Whatever you want, it's yours." I don't think I've ever said truer words.

"Yeah," she says absently. I watch her swallow as she looks down at her clutch. It's awkward, and I don't like it. I don't know what happened between yesterday and today. Whatever it is, I need to fix it.

"Thank you!" Diane practically yells, bouncing in her seat. It takes me a moment to realize she's talking about the beers. Right.

I scratch the back of my head as I head to the cooler and get their drinks. I could fucking use one about now, too.

With two beers in one hand, the glass bottles clinking together, I quickly pop the tops off.

"Charlie!" a customer calls out to me. I wave back, giving them a tight smile but then walk up to James and brush my shoulder against his.

"Take care of them," I instruct, and he follows my eyes to the customer.

"You got it," he says, already moving.

I know I have a rep with these customers. All of them really. But right now, I need time with Grace. Something's not right and I'm not waiting on closing time to put that smile on her face.

I pass Diane the beer and then set Grace's in front of her, but I don't let go. When she tries to grab it, I pull it away, making her tilt her head and smile softly.

I let her have the bottle the second time she reaches for it, mostly because it brings a little happiness to those does eyes of hers. "How's work?" I ask her, and she finally lightens up some.

"I got a promotion," she answers me with a bit of giddiness that makes the nerves settle.

"That's fantastic," I tell her as I toss the caps to the beer in the trash can. "Congrats, sweetheart."

She takes a sip of her beer, still looking a bit nervous.

"You okay-" I start to ask her, but Diane chips in.

"It's really crazy, too. We were sure one of our other co-workers was going to take that job," Diane shakes her head, a look of bewilderment on her face before taking a drink.

My gaze moves to Grace, who's watching Diane with a small frown.

"I have go to the bathroom real quick," Grace doesn't look me in the eyes as she slips off the stool. The air between us is thick and it makes my stomach stir with unease. I don't know what's wrong with her, but I'll find out tonight once everyone leaves. Whatever it is, I'll make it better for her. A sick feeling in my gut is telling me that it's me. *Us.* But I ignore it. We're going to be fine.

I pick up one of the tumblers from the rack and wipe it down before setting it in the clean section and moving to the next glass as Diane switches seats, moving to the stool Grace was just in.

My eyes flick up to her, and I give her a tight smile. I think about asking her if everything's alright with Grace, but I keep my mouth shut, just listening to the sounds of the busy bar.

"So what are you doing tonight?" Diane asks, twirling her hair around her finger. She gives me a seductive smile, and I'm not sure where it's coming from. She knows I'm with Grace. My brows pinch as I think about what to tell her.

Grace. My intentions are to be doing Grace tonight. All night long, if I have any say in the matter.

"Just going home," I answer her tightly. I decide to stay neutral and I assume it's because Diane's drunk that she's acting like this.

"You need company?" she asks.

"I have Grace for that," I bite out the response although I try to keep my voice even and make a move to leave, not liking that I'm in this position at all, but she grabs my hand.

"Not anymore," she says and her answer makes my heart pound. I turn to look at her, not saying a damn thing or changing my expression.

"I mean, she told me it was all fake and she was never really into you like that... it was just for fun," Diane says in a low voice, her hand at the neck of the bottle, tilting it on the bar top. She whispers, leaning in closer. "I get it. You got what you needed from her, and she went slumming for a minute." She pulls back to take a swig of her beer.

My heart feels like a knife's gone through it, slowly twisting and then being pulled out. *She was never into me.* That's all I keep thinking.

No fucking way. Of course she was into me. She wouldn't lie to me. Would she? I move slowly, grabbing a rag from under the bar and wiping down the lacquered wood mindlessly.

"So I was thinking, if you're looking for something tonight-"

"I'm good," my words come out hard and maybe harsh. I don't care though. Diane says something else, but I can't hear anything over the sound of the blood rushing in my ears as I walk away, right to the back of the bar.

My heart's hammering, my blood's boiling. I feel tense and ready to break.

It was fake. Just like my last relationship.

I'm a fucking fool.

Chapter
TWENTY-SEVEN

Grace

I slip onto the barstool next to Diane, deciding to woman up. I want Charlie, and at the very least I can put my heart on the line. Diane looks at me as I right myself, giving me a half smile.

"Hey," I say. I should thank her for convincing me to come although I'm sure she really does just want to get wasted. The booze here is way cheaper than anywhere else around.

"Hey yourself." She sips amber liquid from a rocks glass. Guess she finished her beer already.

Putting my clutch on the bar, I search for Charlie, but the bar's empty.

"Where'd Charlie go?" I ask Diane. I can still feel the awkward tension between us. I just need to spit it out.

She shrugs. "He's around. I think the other bartender is here now, though."

Other bartender? I wonder.

The double doors to the back swing open and grab my attention. Maggie makes an appearance, hauling a big bucket full of ice. She dumps it in the well behind the bar, then hides the bucket. Oh, the *other girl*. I get what Diane's saying now.

"You want something to drink?" Maggie asks. "Charlie's finishing up some stuff in the back."

I glance down to where my beer was when I left and then over to the two empty bottles in front of Diane. "A glass of white zinfandel pretty please."

She pours the wine and sets the glass down in front of me, and all the while it's quiet. My eyes keep flickering back up to the doors. I feel like I need to get these words out now and go tell him, but I can't force myself to interrupt him.

"Wanna go somewhere else?" Diane asks.

Already? We literally just got here. I take her in before answering. She's drunk, or well on her way there. I can tell by her almost-slurred speech, her rumpled clothes.

"No," I say, firming my resolve to talk to Charlie. "I'm going to hang out here for a while longer." I'm careful as I tell her, "If you want to go though, that's fine."

"Whatever," Diane says. I knew she'd take it offensively, but I don't mean it like that. She's just simply had too much to drink.

"You want me to call a cab for you?" I offer.

"I'll get an Uber," she rolls her eyes and snatches her clutch before pushing off of the stool.

"You need help?" I ask her, but she makes a face and turns away from me.

"Hey, Diane." God, I feel horrible. I turn in my seat, but she yells out, "I'm fine," and keeps moving.

I try to shake off the feeling that I should go help Diane.

I really don't want to. She's a grown woman… and kind of a bitch. The last thought makes me relax some as I sip my wine.

My anxiety comes back every time I eye the double doors. I keep my butt planted right where I am and wait for him.

It's now or never. I guess I'm going with option 1 after all.

Time moves slowly as it ticks by. Maggie's in and out and so is the other bartender, I forget his name. Customers start to dwindle and that sick feeling grows in my stomach. I check my phone here and there. Charlie knows I'm here. The feeling that he's ignoring me is growing stronger. I shake out the tension and sip my wine. It's practically room temperature now, but I don't care. I had too many glasses before I came here anyway.

The bar grows quieter and quieter and time keeps going until my phone tells me it's closing time. It's just me and Maggie, although she's in the back with Charlie now. I look around the empty bar and get the urge to go back there, but I don't. He knows I'm here.

After a while, Charlie and Maggie both come back out front. Charlie sees me, and a little bit of a frown crosses his face.

"Hey, I got this," he tells Maggie. Although he's speaking to her, his eyes never leave mine. The way he says it makes my stomach turn.

Maggie slides me a questioning look. "Sure thing, boss."

A few seconds later, the back door bangs shut as she heads out.

Charlie and I are alone.

"I'm supposed to be closing…" he says, walking around the bar. He sits on the barstool next to mine.

"I know. I just… I wanted to see you. Maybe I can help you close?"

He looks at me for a long second, then holds out his hand.

"Come here," he says, pulling me closer to him. I feel the air change between us, and his expression shows something I've never seen before.

"You okay?" I ask him, suddenly feeling like he's breaking up with me. Which is ridiculous, because there's nothing to break up. *Stupid girl.* I knew this would happen. I just don't want it to happen right now. I take it all back. I won't pressure him for anything. Just don't leave me Charlie.

"You like being with me?" he asks me, and I'm quick to nod my head.

"I really do, and-" my voice is tight as I prepare for the worst.

Before I can finish, he kisses me fiercely, spearing his hands in my long hair. His hands are everywhere, running down to touch my breasts, skimming around to touch my ass.

He breaks the kiss, breathing heavy. Oh thank God.

A smile full of relief is pressed against his lips as I kiss him again and again feeling as though each time brings me closer to telling him what I need. I pull his shirt off over his head, tossing it aside. He lets me. His eyes are clouded by something else and that tension is still present between us. I don't stop though. I undo his belt, kissing down his body as I go, trying to show him how much I love being with him.

He inhales sharply, pulling at me not to go down on him.

I'm not about to let him stop me though, so I push against him with my body, and turn him so he's the one facing the bar.

Finally, he relents, helping me and his cock stands proud. Slipping my hand around it, I stroke him, wanting him to know I can give pleasure too. Just like he gave me in that coat closet.

"Grace," he warns, staring at me with a look like this isn't a good idea, but I don't stop.

When I run my tongue from the base of his cock to the very tip, he makes a sound of pent-up longing. I take him in my mouth, inch by inch, but it isn't enough.

He growls and pushes my head down a little, always needing to be the one in control.

Using my tongue against the sensitive underside of his cock, I do everything I can to give him the same kind of pleasure he gave me. Alternating between doing that and taking him deep, it's only minutes before he pulls me away.

At my protest, he merely shakes his head. "There's time for that later. I promise."

Then he pulls me to my feet, switching our positions again. He makes quick work of my dress, pulling it up over my head. I'm not wearing a bra with this dress, so my bare breasts are exposed. I bite my lip as he palms them; heat spreads through my body.

"So beautiful," he marvels. He bends down and takes one nipple in his mouth. He sucks on it, making my back arch. When he releases it in favor of the other, I call out his name.

"Please, Charlie," I moan.

"Please what?" he asks in a low voice with a hint of desperation. Like he needs me to tell him. Like his world depends on it.

"Please..." *Be with me. Be with me for more than just this.* My heart is desperate for me to say the words, but nothing comes out.

The brush of his fingers against my core is like a live wire. He bends to kiss my breast again, his fingers coaxing, opening me to his view.

I moan as he kisses his way down to my pussy. He kneels, discovering me with a series of slow licks that send me sky high.

198

He shifts himself, pressing one hand on the top of my sex, while the other explores.

Charlie finds my clit with his tongue, running lazy circles around it, driving me wild. One finger dips inside my core.

"Yes," I whisper, urging him on.

That same finger that dipped into my center withdraws, then brushes backward.

Is he—?

He chooses that moment to focus on my clit, while sliding his finger around and around the tight hole. I am crazed with the need to get off, and when he focuses in on my clit again, and presses his finger against my rear entrance...

His finger slips in with little resistance. I feel my face heat as I realize that I don't hate it... in fact, it feels... *good.* Hot and full, but it feels so good. Oh my God. It takes everything not to move against his motions.

He slows his pace, giving me a second to get used to the feeling of his finger in my ass, grinding in rhythm. I'm ashamed to find how much I like it. I moan every time he moves his finger.

It's so *taboo*, so wrong...

He sucks on my clit, although I can't forget about where his finger is. He picks up the pace, his tongue moves faster, massaging and taking me higher. He slowly brings a second finger to join the first.

I explode, riding high on a wave of sensation that won't stop. I call his name as I find a sudden release, a blessing or a curse, I don't know.

Before I even finish, Charlie stands up and turns me around. My naked breasts touch the bar and I spread my legs for him. He runs his hand down my bare back, and squeezes one of my ass cheeks.

"You really want me?" he asks me.

"Yes," I *groan*. "Are you going to..." I want to ask him if he's going to try to put himself...

"Not tonight, sweetheart. I don't want to hurt you." Before I can answer, the words are knocked out of me.

He enters me in one brutal stroke, making us both cry out. He fills me completely, possesses me utterly, steals my very breath.

He does it again, and again. Over and over, he strokes into me with every bit of his strength. My body knows what's coming. I'm shaking like a leaf.

Every nerve ending cries out for fulfillment. I move with him, thrust with him until I can't anymore. Until I see the edge of the precipice, looking up from down below.

He doesn't stop fucking me, taking me even higher. Prolonging the pleasure.

He stiffens and grabs my hips hard, bruising my flesh as he finds his own release.

When he's finished, we stand, both catching our breath and coming back down to earth for a long moment, struggling to breathe. I turn my head back, and he nuzzles my neck, but he won't look me in the eyes. He finally withdraws from my body and I wince, already aching between my legs.

"Wait here," he says, pulling up his pants.

I turn around, picking my dress up from the floor. He returns as I'm putting the dress on. He has a clean, wet rag.

"Here," he says, reaching low to wipe the stickiness from between my legs. I balance myself by gripping onto his shoulder as I feel the warm rag wipe me clean.

"Thanks," I say awkwardly. The tension is still there. It's suffocating. As soon as he's done, I finish getting dressed, pulling my panties on and watching Charlie. But he never looks at me the whole time.

I'm trying to be what he wants but I can feel him already slipping away.

He tosses the rag aside and catches me by the waist. Finally, his green eyes stare back at me and my heart flips. His mouth kicks up, half a smile on his face. He kisses me, slow and tender.

When I break away, his smile falters and he lets me go. "I still have to close. It's going to be awhile. An hour, at least." He scratches the back of his head, looking away.

"Oh," I respond but so many questions linger at the back of my throat. "I think I'll go. I have to work in the morning."

"Right," he says with a frown. "Right, of course. I'll just walk you to the door then."

"No need," I assure him. "I think I can make it a whole hundred feet alone."

He looks like he's going to argue with me, but then he swallows it back. "Sure. I'll see you later, then?" he asks.

"Yeah. Sure," I answer him as I slip on my heels, only then remembering I never told him anything I wanted to say. It hurts way too much to not be a breakup.

"Okay. Text me when you get home, let me know you got there safe."

I give him a half smile that I don't mean, feeling the split between us. *What the hell is wrong with me?*

I open my mouth to tell him, but I can't. He has to work, and I need to get home. If I say anything right now, I know I'm going to cry. I'm going to be that clingy girl he didn't want. Instead, I let myself out and cry alone in the car on my way home alone.

Chapter
TWENTY-EIGHT

Charlie

Little Evie is upright in Joseph's lap, staring back at me with wide eyes as I shove peas into my mouth.

I don't taste a damn thing. It's been five days. *Five fucking days since that night at the bar.*

I should have ended it that night at the bar or at least told her I knew what she told Diane. I should have told her no, but I just wanted to feel her one last time. Five days and she hasn't said a word to me. Hasn't come by. She never wanted a relationship with me.

I'm so fucking pathetic, wrapped up in a woman who doesn't want me. Who never wanted me. I remember how she tried to get out of it. I should have let her.

I'm so fucking stupid.

My fork clinks on the ceramic plate as I lower my head, feeling like shit.

"How long is their trip?" Cheryl asks Ma. It's just Cheryl, Joseph, Ma and Pops while Ali and Michael are on their honeymoon. Without Ali here, it's quieter than usual. Or maybe I just think it is.

"A full week," Ma answers, taking a sip of her Diet Pepsi and shifting in her seat.

"Oh wow," Cheryl says, absently kissing the top of Evie's head, although the little girl still stares back at me. "That's a long honeymoon."

"We can go on another," Joseph pipes up then shovels another bite in his mouth.

Cheryl scoffs, leaning back in her seat and yawning before she says, "Like when the kids are in college?"

Joseph starts to answer, but Ma cuts in, "*Kids?*" Her eyes flicker to Cheryl's stomach.

"Oh don't get ahead of yourself, Ma." Cheryl stretches one arm over her head, another yawn taking over as she does.

"Just checking," Ma says with a smile. Pops chuckles at the end of the table. He's been quiet all night but keeps looking at me. He thinks I don't notice, but I do. They're all looking at me, and I'm just waiting for the questions to start.

As if reading my mind, Ma asks, "When are you going to bring Grace to dinner, Charlie?" She picks up a bun from the basket all the while looking at me, waiting on my answer.

I lean back in my seat, taking in a heavy breath.

If I call her, I think she'd answer. If I ask her to come by, I think she would.

She's busy with the promotion, and I've got work, too. I want to give in and just get lost in her touch, but it's turning into something else for me. I never should've asked her to come around after the wedding.

I'm ashamed to say how much it hurts to end it with her. I don't want to, but I can't forget what Diane told me and it just makes sense. I'm not the man she wants her happily ever after with. We both knew that from the beginning.

I don't want to believe Diane, but she knew it was fake. She said that word, *fake*. That had to have come from Grace. There's no other way Diane could have known it was some stupid drunken deal and we were pretending.

"She's real busy," I say before taking a drink of my water. "She got a promotion."

"Oh that's wonderful," Ma answers, but her tone is flat and I keep my head down to avoid looking at her.

"Just where'd you two run off to during the reception?" Joseph asks me, and when I look up I see his cocky smile as he picks off a piece of his chicken and pops it into his mouth.

"Nowhere," I answer him as Cheryl shoves her elbows into his side. She gives him a look, and little Evie finally looks away from me and up to her mom. She's only a few months old, but she's holding her head up just fine and staring at the world around her with wonder.

I'm not fucking settling. And not on a woman who doesn't want me. For the first time since it happened, I regret thinking about knocking Grace up. My heart clenches in my chest, and I take another gulp of my water.

I don't know what got into me with her, but I know it needs to end.

I made a mistake, and not for the first time. But I'm damn sure not going to let history repeat itself.

"Son, help me with something." Ma's request is odd, especially coming in the middle of dinner. Just like her calling me 'son' is throwing me off.

"Of course," I answer her, setting my napkin to the side

and following her to the kitchen. She keeps walking, out to the back door and to the patio.

"What do you need help with out here?"

My Ma's a bit shorter than me and when she takes a seat on the floral tufted cushion, she's even shorter. Taking my cue, I have a seat on the chair opposite her. "I need you to tell me what's wrong."

"Nothing's wrong," I do my best to appease her and whatever hints she has that I'm off.

"That's not true. Mickey told me Grace hasn't been in. Maggie said she thinks you two got in a fight.

What in the ever loving hell. My eyes must speak my thought for me. "Don't look at me like that," my mother scolds me. "They're worried for you," she stresses and my mom's voice shakes.

"She doesn't want to be with me," I explain, getting right to the point and looking at my mother and saying those words makes the truth hurt even more.

"Bull," my mother bites out, her eyes getting glassy. "I saw the way she looks at you and the way you look at her," my mom's hands clasp in her lap, almost like she's praying. "You tell me what happened and I'll tell you how to fix it."

"I don't need you getting us back together. I'll settle down and find a nice girl one day." My throat gets tight and I can't finish my thoughts. Mostly about how my mother doesn't have to worry like she is.

"Didn't I love you enough to know what it feels like?" she asks me, a tear escaping and I lean forward, reaching for my mother's hand. She shakes it away from me and wipes her eyes. "You love her and she loves you and this isn't okay. I know Suzanne hurt you but you deserve love and I don't know why you don't fight for it."

"She doesn't want me," I emphasize as kindly as I can to my emotional mother.

"Son, if you think I didn't pick up on the fact that you were only friends before, you must think I'm a fool. That first day I met her, I knew you two lied."

"Ma, I-"

"Hush, boy," she cuts me off. "I let it go because I could tell she wanted you. She had her eye set on you like I did your father. If you were blind to that, I can forgive it. But I can't forgive you thinking she doesn't love you. Not when everyone around you knows she does."

She doesn't get it and it kills me. I hate feeling like this. I hate seeing my mother like this even more.

"Do you love her?"

I hesitate only a second before answering, "yes."

"Did you tell her?"

Swallowing the lump in my throat, I answer my mother. "No."

"Just promise me this. You'll tell her how you feel. How you really feel." She nods slowly as if agreeing to whatever she's thinking.

What it is, I don't know.

"Promise me, Charlie."

"I promise, I'll tell her." When I answer my mom, I don't think much of it. But the more I think about it, the more I know I don't have anything to lose. She's already gone, it can only bring her back to me.

Chapter
TWENTY-NINE

Grace

You're pregnant, the doctor's voice echoes in my head. *Congratulations, Grace.*

I grip the steering wheel as I drive home, willing myself not to cry. It's a mix of happiness, wonder and profound sadness. Charlie gave me a baby.

Four days past the supposed day I was supposed to get my period, AKA yesterday, I peed on a stick and then cried. I told Ann, who's immediate response was: you have to tell him. I almost told my mother, but it's so soon. So to the doctor's I went, who, surprisingly also only had me pee on a stick.

Take it easy and be happy. Those were the good doctor's only words of advice.

I have to tell him. Ann's right. But how? It's been a week. He messaged yesterday that we had to talk. Everyone knows what those words mean and then… I took the test.

How can I look a man in the eyes and tell him I'm pregnant when the words out of his mouth are that he doesn't want to see me anymore?

With a right turn onto my street, I come around the corner, and I'm surprised to find Charlie. Fate is cruel. I couldn't have had one more day before I have to face this?

Just one day of looking up cribs and searching for three-bedroom houses. Making plans and checklists and searching baby names and their meanings.

Deep breath in. He's sitting on the steps to my building. Deep breath out and he sees me as I pull into my designated parking spot.

There isn't a pep talk in the world that will prepare me so all I do is grab my purse and get the hell out to face him.

I imagine what I'll blurt out:

I really liked you and even fell for you and you hurt me.

I miss you and if I hurt you, I'm sorry.

… also. I'm pregnant and I swear I wasn't lying when I told you I didn't think it was possible.

Shit… shit, shit, shit. I can't say that to him. What if he really does think I'm a liar? What if he thinks I used him? Oh my God, I just can't take this.

"You didn't answer my calls or texts," Charlie explains before I'm even six feet from him. He's already standing, right in the center of the path.

I stare at him for a long moment, at his downcast expression and his regretful posture. He usually takes up all the space around him, but now he's meek.

Sweeping my hand out, which causes my purse to fall off my shoulder, I gesture toward the doorway. "Do you want to come in?" My heart is frantic, although outwardly I'm trying not to show it. It feels like it's all just too little too late. Too many days passed. Too many truths weren't shared. This is where it all implodes.

"I... I have something I wanted to tell you," I admit to him and it takes all the air in my lungs to do it.

Charlie ambles inside not taking his eyes off me, and I close the door behind us both. The click seems louder than usual. I put my keys down in the bowl and hang up my purse, then walk over to where Charlie has seated himself on the edge of the couch.

I look at him for a second, then sit on the bed, my butt pushing back my pillows.

"Talk to me," he says.

"About what?" Nervousness pricks at the back of my neck. Does he already know?

"Just... tell me what's going on in that head of yours. I want to know."

Thump. "You sure?" I ask like a silly naïve girl.

"Really. Even if it's all bad stuff about me, I want to know. I want you to get it out."

His eyes plead with me, and I know I have to tell him. I can't hide this from him, not with him here, asking what I'm thinking. I need to be strong and tell him what happened. I look down at the comforter, swallowing thickly and picking at the threads.

"I feel like you broke up with me even though we weren't together," the words slip out before I can catch them.

"We were together and I don't want to break up."

"I thought... I meant-" I start to say, but he cuts me off.

"You mean more to me than I told you. You do. You mean a lot to me."

"Why did you—" I can't even place what he did or what happened that made me feel that way. "Maybe I just got in my head or—"

"No. I'm sorry, Grace." He holds my gaze, and I feel it. I feel his sincerity. "I pushed you away and I'm sorry. I meant something to you too, right? You did want me?" he questions like he doesn't know the answer.

"Of course I did. I still do. I don't think I could ever not want you." Surprise catches me in its grip, watching the relief roll through his shoulders.

It's quiet for a long time, the sound of my heart beating faster and faster filling my ears. *Tell him. Tell him about the pregnancy.*

"You told Diane it was fake—"

"Diane?" her name comes out like a curse from my mouth as my ass pops off the bed. "What the hell did she tell you?"

"It doesn't—"

"The hell it doesn't matter!" I could kill her right now. What right did she have to come between Charlie and me?

Charlie doesn't have patience for my reaction. "Listen to me Grace. Just listen to me."

With his pleading words, I carefully sit back down, the bed creaking in the silence and I make a mental note to never speak to Diane again unless it has to do with work. She's not my friend. There needs to be a boundary between her and I and I'm the one who has to set it. Gesturing for Charlie to continue, I wait for what he has to say before I tell him the whole truth.

"It doesn't really matter because I shouldn't have listened to her. I should have asked you. I thought it was over. And I'm sorry. But I want you, and I care for you...." His words are genuine and sincere.

"Wait. Wait." I stop him and try to remember every thought I had last night. How he doesn't have to be with me because I'm pregnant. How he can be in the baby's life or not.

210

"I want to tell you something first... I..." I have to suck in a deep breath and stare at the ceiling to tell him. "I'm pregnant," I say. Even though I thought I cried all the tears earlier, my eyes well up.

Charlie blinks a few times. "What?"

"I swear I didn't think I could..." I can't breathe as Charlie stands, his brow knit and he comes around the sofa, closer to my bed. My heart pounds.

"When did you find out?" he questions and in the million ways I imagined telling him that was never a question he asked. "Yesterday. I promise I didn't know that it would happen when I said no condom... I swear," I practically stutter as Charlie gets closer, his gaze intense and the air around him seeming to bend everything else, blurring it.

"I just came from the doctor and it's obviously early and..." I don't know what to say when he looks at me like that. With that sharp piercing gaze.

"Do you love me?" he questions me, now only inches away. The heat from his body wraps around me. My fingers dig into the comforter to ground me as I crane my neck to look up at him. He towers over me and my heart beats loudly in my ears.

"Of course I do." Tears prick my eyes. I almost add, it's okay if you don't love me back. I'm so close, so desperate to be okay with whatever he wants because he makes me so happy and he's the only piece in the puzzle of life that's missing for me. I'll take him anyway I can get. *Please don't leave me.* I want to beg him. I'm shamelessly in love with him and he's all I want.

"Good. Lay down sweetheart," Charlie whispers, cupping my chin and kissing me just once, soft and sweet. A fluttering in my chest tells me it's okay. With both of my hands wrapped around his, I lift my lips, stealing another kiss.

Before I can do as he wishes, he lowers his lips to my ear and confesses, "I want to make love to you."

There are so many questions, so many decisions to make, but right now, that's all I want. I want him to make love to me. I want nothing more than for him to love me.

Chapter
THIRTY

Charlie

It's not the sunlight that wakes me. It's not my alarm clock, or the nagging feeling in the pit of my stomach. It's the instant knowledge that she's in my arms.

Maybe I was dreaming of her, I don't know. But in one second, I knew it was real, she was here and I had to wake up. I had to be awake to take her in and make sure I still had her.

I lost her once, and I'll never lose her again.

Never.

She shifts slightly, her soft body going a bit stiff. I can feel the warmth from her, but there's space between us.

Too much space.

Especially knowing… she loves me. My heart clenches as I wrap my arm around her and pull her closer to me. Nestling her ass right where it belongs, up against me. I lean forward, planting a kiss on her slender neck and waiting for her to turn to face me.

The sheets rustle as she shifts slightly and then rolls fully in my arms so we're face to face. Those beautiful lips of hers turn up slightly, but it's a sad smile.

"Charlie," she starts, her eyes falling to the pillow as she pushes her messy hair out of her face.

"Whatever you want to hear, I'll say it." My voice is flat and hard, leaving no room for negotiation. Her eyes dart up to mine with a flash of something, something that's gone before I can recognize it.

"What?" Her eyes search mine as she takes in a slow breath.

I try to steady my own breathing, wanting nothing more than to take her right here and now, but her eyes are holding me in place. They see through me, willing me to give her more.

"I want you," I breathe my answer. I've never wanted someone or something so damn much. Nothing more than I want her right here, right now.

"For what?" there's a vulnerability in her eyes as she swallows thickly and adds, "Why? Not because you feel obligated—"

"Stop. No, that's not why. Don't ever think that," I answer quickly, not wanting her to ever get that idea in her head.

"You don't understand," her voice wavers and she shakes her head slightly, the wind brushing the hair from her face. "You want this, just what we have right now." She says the words like it's a bad thing.

"Of course I do."

"I want you anyway I can have you. Like this, with a baby, with no baby. I'm so willing to… I don't know how to explain it but it… It doesn't… I don't want to force you into something or be with someone… who…"

I cup her head with the back of my hand, waiting for her look at me. "Grace. I can't tell you what I will want a year from now. Shit, I don't even know what I'll want a month from now, but I'll want you in my life. *I want you.*"

"I want you, but I want a family, too. I just wish it hadn't happened like this and the last time I saw you…" Her voice carries the same no-bullshit attitude as mine and she holds my gaze.

My heart beats loud in my chest and I swallow thickly, still holding her gaze.

I lick my lips, feeling my pulse race as I splay my hand on her lower back and pull her close to me. "I was a fool and I'm sorry. But I'm here now; I'm not leaving and I don't want you to walk away from me."

"I don't want to walk away." Grace huffs a sad laugh, shaking her head. "But you know me. And I know you," she swallows, her voice cracking. "And if it's not what you want… then we can work something else out and I'll survive." Tears form in her eyes and I shush her, rubbing her back and kissing her forehead.

She doesn't stop, she lets it all out. "I love you and if this stays the way it is… I know I'll let it be whatever you want it to be. I'll let time go by. I'll let you never commit to me. I'll be sacrificing something I may never be able to have, and I'll regret it. And Charlie, I want this baby. I'm so damn sorry, but I want a family too," she wipes her nose with the back of her hand and then under her eyes with her fingers, all the while shaking her head. "I love you, but I want a family. I want a loving family. I don't want to trap you or…"

I pull her back some by her shoulders so she can look at

me as I say, "I want a wife, I want a baby. I want to fill my house with pictures of my kids and clutter from all those little toys."

She's still wiping away tears as I add, "Come move in with me. Let's try this for real." It's not fucking around or a game, or pretend or a stupid drunken deal. I want to put my all into this, for her and for our future.

"Not for any other reason than to see if we can make this work?" she asks me. Right then and right there, I know how the rest of my life is going to be. She's going to be right by my side if I can help it. I know with everything in me that we will make it work. Because she wants this and so do I. It's easy between us. It always was. I was the reason we were apart. If I give her this, it's over. I'm done for. She'll have me wrapped around her finger and knocking her up again in no time. I search her eyes and all I see there is love.

It's what I feel for her, too.

"I already know we work Grace. You're my sweetheart." I answer her with the only truth I know. "I want to be with you and that's the only answer there is. I love you, Grace."

Chapter

THIRTY-ONE

Grace

Unwrapping a stack of plates, I move from the living room into the open-concept kitchen. The theme of this room must be gray, because the appliances, the countertops, and even the cabinets are gray and smooth. I set the plates down and open all the cabinets, searching for the place where the plates belong.

I find them in the last cabinet I open, far away from Charlie's stove and refrigerator. Picking up my plates, I sigh as I move them into the cupboard. This is the third area of Charlie's house I've found to be disorganized while in the process of moving my stuff in. Thankfully, he's fine with me moving everything around. Like, actually good with it. He didn't just say it to appease me, which is what I was afraid of. Most of the house was empty, with all of my things in here now, it's... well it's still a bit bare. We'll make this house a home though. Charlie tells me that every night.

With a pleasant warmth running through me, I shut the cabinet door softly and count the days again. It's been almost a month. I'm exhausted, which is apparently normal for the first trimester, but more than that, I'm still in awe that this is really my life.

I got the Prince Charming I longed for. My hand slips to my lower belly. Together, we'll have a family.

Sooner or later, I'm going to break down and reorganize the kitchen, the bathroom, and the laundry room. I would do it now, but I don't want to freak Charlie out... although Ann says when I start nesting, I won't have much of a choice.

Back to the living room, I pick up the now-empty box that previously held the plates. Breaking it down, I fold it flat so it will be easier to take out to the recycling later.

My phone buzzes in the back pocket of my jeans and I pull it out to check the message. It's a text from Charlie, saying he'll be home soon... and that I better not be lifting anything heavy. The last part makes me laugh. I might be tired, but it's not like I'm suddenly frail and can't lift a couple of dishes.

My phone vibrates in my hand. I check it again, and then grin. It's a picture of Eric, Charlie's new bar manager, standing on his hands on top of the bar. Eric is supposed to manage the bar in Charlie's stead, but Charlie's having a hard time letting go.

I guess it's safe to leave Mac's in this guy's hands... right? he texts.

I'm pretty sure. You wouldn't have hired him otherwise. I respond.

Okay. On my way home.

I check the time, and realize it's midnight, long past my bedtime. I got wrapped up with unpacking, but I'll still be expected at work in the morning.

At my new position. In my new office. Oh, and a Diane-free office at that. She got fired. When Sarah informed me, I didn't even bother asking why. I just told her I'd divide her assignments accordingly. *Good riddance.* Ann agrees. When I told Ann what happened at Mac's that night, she flipped on Diane.

I drift into Charlie's bedroom, shaking off the negativity —*our bedroom*, I suppose I should call it. Only good vibes from here on out. For both Charlie and me. Taking a seat on the edge of the bed and feeling a yawn come over me, I look down at my grubby t-shirt and cotton shorts. It'll only take a moment to change out of these and into a button down of Charlie's to greet him in when he comes home. It only takes a moment and I'm glad I did. The cotton smells just like him.

It's been a hell of a month. I moved all my things into Charlie's two-story McMansion. It's out in the rural area, and I absolutely love it. Charlie and some of his guy friends helped move all the big stuff so it only took one day.

I'm surprised there weren't raised eyebrows and red alarm bells from his family and friends. And judging by the comments from his sisters and mother, when we finally tell them we're pregnant, at that safe twelve-week mark, I think they're going to be overjoyed. I love my mother, but a big family is different. I didn't know how much love could be amplified.

The metallic chime of the security system alerts me that somebody opened the front door. I huddle under the covers, waiting for him. He's going to shower before he joins me, and I'll probably drift asleep. But he always kisses me first thing.

When he comes around the corner, I can't control the smile that breaks out across my face. He looks so handsome, in his old Mac's t-shirt and low slung jeans with a peek of that sexy "V" showing.

He's all mine. My sexy southern bartender to knock boots with.

"Looks like you went through a good number of boxes in the living room," he says, jerking his thumb over his shoulder as he comes into the room.

"I made a decent dent," I sigh.

He comes over to the bed, eyeing me. He swoops down and kisses me. The faint smell of beer follows him.

"You look like you could fall right asleep." he comments and then does just want I knew he would. Plants a kiss right on my lips.

"I don't know," I only answer once he breaks the kiss. "Maybe?" Right after the word is spoken, I involuntarily yawn.

"I guess that answers my question," he says with a rough chuckle, winking at me and heading to the master bath.

"No, wait," I say, tugging his arm. "Tell me something. I don't want to fall asleep without talking a little bit."

He looks at me for a long moment, then shakes his head.

"What?" I ask.

"I was going to wait until you're more awake, but..."

He reaches in his back pocket and pulls out a Ring Pop. Scrunching my face curiously, I watch as he gets off the bed, kneeling on the floor.

"What are you doing?" I ask with a stupid grin on my face. *A Ring Pop?*

"Asking you to marry me, if you don't mind."

My mouth falls open and my heart thumps loud and fast. I stare at him, and he looks back at me, the hint of a smile on his face. But also nervousness. Holy shit. No he's not really. Goosebumps break out over my body.

"You're kidding," I accuse.

"I'm not. I'm just waiting for a sign that you want to hear the words."

"I… I…" I try to answer with my lungs refusing to work.

My throat closes up, and tears threaten. I am officially speechless. I manage a nod.

"Yes? You want to hear them?"

I nod again.

"I love you, Grace Campbell. I don't want to lose you ever again. I want to build a life with you. I want us to have a family, together."

Yes. Those are exactly the words I want to hear. That thudding in my chest gets harder and I watch him pull a small black velvet box from his back pocket, the opposite one that the Ring Pop was in.

My eyes prick with tears and I sit up straighter.

He pauses. I press my fingers to my lips. I can't believe this is really happening.

"It's been in my back pocket for almost a week now, Grace. I wanted it to be perfect. I want everything to be perfect for you. For us."

"Charlie," all I can say is his name.

"Grace, will you marry me?" Charlie asks, looking at me with those soulful green eyes.

I launch myself off the bed, tackling him. My kisses land more on his face than his mouth, but Charlie doesn't seem to mind.

When the kisses taper off, he slides the diamond onto my finger, the ring sparkling and shining bright. It's a large diamond, I don't know how many carats, but it sits perfect on my finger.

Charlie chuckles. "You approve?"

"I love it," I answer, brushing the tears from my face.

"So tell me what I want to hear."

"The kissing and tackling weren't evidence enough?" I tease.

"Not for me," he says, his eyes sparkle and the smile on his face widens. "Not when it's something this important."

I lean in and kiss him tenderly. "Yes, Charlie. I want to marry you."

"Good. Because I want to do this with you forever. I'm all in."

"Forever?" I question.

"Forever," he repeats.

"I love you, Grace."

"I love you too, Charlie."

Epilogue

Charlie

The sound of keys tapping rattles through the house. Grace is busy at work again. I roll in the bed onto my side and stare at the digital red numbers, 4:33 a.m.

The bed groans as I shift my weight and crawl out of bed. My sweetheart's been getting into this habit lately. It started before the wedding when she knew she'd be taking time off.

And now she's at it again.

Ever since she was promoted and in charge of her own team, she works nonstop. Well, mostly. But just like me, we make time for each other.

My wedding band clinks on the doorknob as I open the bedroom door wider and follow the soft clicks of her laptop in the office.

I lean against the doorframe, resting my head there and watching her for a moment.

She's made my house a home. Leaving work is now enjoyable, knowing that I'm coming home to her beautiful smile.

The faint light from her computer bathes her in a glow. My lips creep up into a smile. No, that glow is from something else.

As my eyes travel to her swollen belly, the tapping of her laptop stops.

Her gorgeous blue eyes stare back at me as she asks, "Did I wake you?" A wrinkle sets in the middle of her forehead as she frowns and gets up to come over to me. Her belly almost pushes against the desk, but she turns in time. She's only now getting used to the weight of our little boy.

Six months pregnant, a little over a month after marriage, almost a year since I first laid eyes on her, and I couldn't love her more.

Our baby boy is healthy, and the doctors don't expect any complications. It's funny how she was so nervous and anxious, but the moment she got pregnant, she relaxed and I became the one who was worrying about everything.

I open my arms as she slowly walks to me, the lack of sleep seeming to hit her as she reaches me.

Her soft body molds to mine as I hold her and kiss her hair. The smell of her shampoo tickles my nose as I smile. "I missed you I think," my words reflect my sleepy state. "I can't sleep when you're not in bed."

She lifts her head to look at me, "I just wanted to get this one done before the baby comes."

My smile only widens at her response. "We have three more months, sweetheart."

She pouts in response, and it only makes me want to kiss her that much more.

Her lips part to give some excuse, but I don't let her say a word. I crush my lips to hers, spearing my fingers through her hair and deepening it when she melts into me.

A year since I set eyes on her, and I don't know how I ever lived without her.

When I pull away from her, Grace's hands travel toward her belly and I know why; I can feel our little boy kicking her. She looks up at me in wonder, as if it's the first time she's felt him.

A chuckle escapes me as I push her hair out of her face and plant a chaste kiss on her lips.

She grabs my hand and places it on her belly and our baby kicks my hand just then. It's hard enough that I would have pulled back had Grace's hand not still been on top of mine.

"Is he why you can't sleep?" I ask her playfully, my hands traveling over her swollen bump.

"No, the lavender pillow spray works really well to put me out." My eyes reach hers again, and in them I see nothing but happiness. Cheryl has been over nonstop, giving her all sorts of things.

Grace happened to say once at Sunday dinner that she wasn't sleeping well. The very next day my sisters and mom were over here with all sorts of pillows and aromatherapy sprays. My Ma knew. She knows everything.

I've never loved my family more than now. And I know Grace loves them, too.

Together, we're complete; there's no doubt in my mind that this is how it was supposed to happen all along.

I tip her chin up, holding her gaze for a moment before kissing her one last time and whispering, "I love you." I can feel her smile on my lips before she whispers back, "And I love you."

About the
AUTHOR

Thank you so much for reading my romances. I'm just a stay at home mom and avid reader turned author and I couldn't be happier.

I hope you love my books as much as I do!

More by Willow Winters
www.willowwinterswrites.com/books

Made in the USA
Middletown, DE
30 September 2023